Clare Connelly wa[s] [born] amongst a family of [book lovers, some] of her childhood up [with a book in] hand. Clare is marri[ed to a Frenchman] and they live in a bungalow near the sea with their two children. She is frequently found staring into space—a sure-fire sign that she's in the world of her characters. She has a penchant for French food and ice-cold champagne, and Mills & Boons continue to be her favourite ever books. Writing for Mills & Boon is a long-held dream. Clare can be contacted via clareconnelly.com or her Facebook page.

J. Margot Critch currently lives in St John's, Newfoundland, with her husband, Brian, and their two little buddies, Simon and Chibs. She spends equal amounts of time writing, listening to Jimmy Buffett's music and looking out at the ocean—all the while trying to decide if she wants coffee or a margarita.

If you liked *Burn Me Once* and
Boardroom Sins, why not try

Pleasure Games by Daire St. Denis
Legal Attraction by Lisa Childs

Discover more at millsandboon.co.uk

BURN ME ONCE

CLARE CONNELLY

BOARDROOM SINS

J. MARGOT CRITCH

MILLS & BOON

First Published in Great Britain 2018
by Mills & Boon, an imprint of HarperCollins*Publishers*
1 London Bridge Street, London, SE1 9GF

Burn Me Once © 2018 Clare Connelly

Boardroom Sins © 2018 Juanita Margot Critch

ISBN: 978-0-263-26643-6

MIX
Paper from
responsible sources
FSC˚ C007454

This book is produced from independently certified FSC™ paper
to ensure responsible forest management.
For more information visit www.harpercollins.co.uk/green.

Printed and bound in Spain
by CPI, Barcelona

BURN ME ONCE

CLARE CONNELLY

MILLS & BOON

For anyone who's ever fallen hard for a muso.
And for Isaac Hanson, who was my first rock star crush.
We'll always have *MMMBop*.

PROLOGUE

In what distant deeps or skies
Burnt the fire of thine eyes?
On what wings dare he aspire?
What the hand, dare seize the fire?
                                        —William Blake

SHE HAS GOT to be kidding me.

I stare at the screen one last time, checking that the Tweet actually exists. And there it is. One hundred and forty characters reaching through time and space to slam me hard over the head.

I'm getting married! @_TheRealTomBanks asked and obv I said yes!!! Couldn't be happier! #soinlove #dreamsdocometrue #happyeverafter

I curl my fingers around my phone, tempted to pitch the damned thing into the street. Only the thought of the personal information I keep stored in it stops me from being so reckless. The press would have a field-day if they found my phone lying in the gutter.

How can she still screw with me even now, three months after we 'took a break'?

Then again, isn't this so like Sienna? Sienna who's had six years of my life. Sienna whom I thought I loved. Sienna who is now engaged to another man.

Fractured memories of our last months together assault me from all angles; they are blades of mirrored glass, shards through my mind, tormenting me every which way, pricking me with exquisite ecstasy.

It was a nightmare.

And yet it was my life.

The nightmare has ended and I don't know if I remember how to live.

I need a drink. And I need to get Sienna the hell out of my head once and for all. And I can think of a really good way to kill two birds with one stone.

The bar is hardly my usual scene. It's retro, but in an authentic way, which I guess means the décor hasn't been updated since the early nineties. There's peeling linoleum in the corner of the bar, where I prop my arms and hunch down, not wanting to attract attention to myself.

#happyeverafter, my ass.

I order a beer, barely noticing the recognition that flickers across the guy's face. I'm used to being recognised. So is Sienna. Which makes it even harder to believe she's been able to keep this relationship secret. Not just from me, but the world.

A frown gravels across my jaw. No, she didn't

keep the whole thing secret. They're *friends*. *Just friends*. She's told me that a dozen times. And I bought it.

Was she fucking him at the same time she was me? Jesus. Was that why she ended it? She told me she needed space to figure herself out and I bought it. Space? *Space?*

After six years together she doesn't even have the fucking decency to give me a heads-up that she's with someone else?

Nausea rolls in my gut.

I don't particularly ascribe to the rock and roll lifestyle, but tonight I want to write myself off. I want to get hammered. I want to get drunk. I want to get fall-down pissed.

I need to forget about Sienna somehow.

CHAPTER ONE

'Come On! It's the perfect opportunity to put Jeremy behind you.'

I send Eliza a look of impatience but can't fight the ever-present swoop of shame that accompanies any mention of his name. 'He *is* behind me.'

'If that were true you wouldn't have spent the past eight months wallowing!'

'I am *not* wallowing,' I deny, turning to Cassie pleadingly.

'I can see why you think I'd back you up, but seriously, Ally, you *have* to get back out there.'

My stomach flops and my gaze wanders towards the man at the bar.

Ethan 'rock star' Ash. And so much hotter in real life than I could ever have imagined.

I shake my head. 'No way. I'm not going to talk to him.'

'Why not?' Cassie throws a look over her shoulder, and when she looks back at us she has a pretty flush in her cheeks.

'Because.' I shoot them both a look they know

better than to argue with. 'Now, can we please talk about something else?'

I sip my drink, crossing my legs in the other direction, and most definitely *not* looking towards the bar again.

'What's new?'

I listen to their responses, relieved as all hell that they've let the matter of the smoking hot rock god drop. At least for now…

'Drinks are empty. It's your turn, Ally.'

I blink, drawn back into the conversation by Eliza, who is handing her glass to me. I frown. 'Isn't it table service?'

'Nah. Not on a Friday.'

I grimace. 'Remind me why we chose this place again?'

Cassie points to the sign overhead and I know what it says without even reading it: *Happy Hour— 9-9!*

As the only one of our little trio who can afford full-price drinks in decent bars with professional wait staff, I resist the urge to complain. Besides, the place is obviously good enough for Ethan Ash. Which begs the question: *what's he doing here?* He's alone, and has been since I got here an hour earlier. Is he waiting for someone? Has he been stood up? That doesn't make sense. Who'd stand *him* up?

I'm two cocktails in, so I know I have a bit of an alcohol-confident swagger as I make my way to the bar. But I'm immune to tall, dark and handsome men now—Jeremy cured me of that habit for life—

so I determinedly move past him—*way* past, like other-planet past—choosing to prop my elbows on a spot that's practically in the kitchen it's so far away from him.

Despite the fact there are at least seven people serving behind the bar, I'm kept waiting for several minutes. Slowing down is probably a good thing, so I don't make a fuss. I pull my phone out instead, flicking through Instagram and checking my emails, humming along without realising to the song overhead. It's only when the song begins to surround, envelop and roll over me, with an oddly perfect surround-sound quality, that I look up and realise he's right beside me.

He.

He of the thick brown hair and ocean-green eyes. He of the tanned skin and gazillion-pack abs. He of the torn jeans and loose grey shirt—designer dishevelled. And the way he smells—delicious. My gut twists in enthusiastic acknowledgement of all of the above and my knees tremble as if they're conspiring to pull me closer to him.

But my face is still following orders and thankfully stays resolutely unimpressed.

A smile flicks his lips as he continues to croon—yes, he's actually *crooning*—the words to a pop song, for God's sake—and I desperately don't want him to stop.

'How's it going?'

It's so completely *not* what I expect he of the

stubbled jaw to say that I laugh softly. 'How's *what* going?'

His grin is disarming and he obviously knows it. How could he not? His accent is huskier in real life—broad British that is more Midlands than Eton. It's sexy AF.

'Life. The universe. Your place in it.'

'Ah. That sounds like a conversation more suited to Neil deGrasse Tyson's living room.'

'Want me to give him a call? See if he's free?'

I roll my eyes. 'Sure. You got him on speed dial or something?'

He lifts his phone out of his pocket. It's an iPhone, I think, but it looks to be pure gold. Catching me looking, he seems almost embarrassed as he clarifies, 'I get given them.'

At that moment, thank God, a waiter appears behind the bar. 'What'll it be?'

'Vodka gimlet, gin and tonic and Prosecco.'

He nods and moves away, picking up where he of the smooth as caramel voice left off, singing the song softly as he mixes our drinks.

'See?'

Ethan calls me back to him and he's holding his phone so I can see the world's most famous astrophysicist staring back at me.

'You seriously know him?'

'Sure. We did a charity thing together a year ago. Nice guy.'

I arch a brow. Am I *really* standing in a bar in

SoHo talking to a veritable rock god superstar about a world-famous scientist?

'I'm impressed.'

'So am I. I think you're the first girl I've met in a bar who outed herself as a science nerd.'

'Your implication being that knowing who one of the most pre-eminent astrophysicists of our time is makes me a nerd? I would think that's kind of mainstream knowledge.'

He shrugs. 'Not in my experience.'

'Ah. So maybe your experience is just...limited.'

The bartender returns with our drinks, and before I can hand my credit card over Ethan Sexier-than-Thou Ash slides his own across the bar.

'Maybe it is.'

His eyes hold mine and my tummy lurches as though I've just driven at speed over the crest of a hill. I'm in free fall.

'Don't use his card,' I say, my voice croaky as I drag my attention to the waiter behind the bar. 'It's my shout.'

'You can get the next round.' Ethan's voice brooks no opposition and the bartender taps his card on the machine.

'Next round?' I arch a brow. 'Meaning...?'

He leans closer. He smells amazing. Like salt and sand and sunshine all rolled into one.

'Meaning these drinks are on me.'

He pulls back just far enough to grin at me while his eyes meet mine, green versus blue, and I am losing whatever battle it is we're waging. Then his fingers lift up and press lightly to the back of my hand. Just for a second, but it's enough. Heat spirals up my arm spreading goosebumps on my flesh and, mortifyingly, tensing my nipples. His eyes catch the reaction and my cheeks flush bright pink.

'It was nice to meet you…?'

His question hangs in the air but I'm flummoxed. The way my body has reacted is strange. Unexpected.

'You too.'

I deliberately don't give him my name. Names are where the problems start.

I'm over Jeremy. I am.

If I ever see him again I think I could seriously find myself in a federal prison for life.

But the ghost of what we were…what he turned me into…is thick inside me. *Always.* I don't remember the last time I looked in the mirror and didn't see *her. That* woman. The woman he made me. The woman I came to loathe.

I fight the shudder. I'm not her any more. But it's taken eight long months to claw my way back, and names are the beginning of forgetting that.

No names.

I lift the three drinks easily between my hands and give him one last smile without meeting his eyes before making my way back to the table.

Eliza and Cassie are staring at me, the former with a knowing smile and the latter with a dropped jaw.

'You *talked* to him?' Cassie squeaks in obvious disbelief.

'He talked to me,' I mumble, sliding their drinks across the table and looking guiltily towards the bar. He's talking to someone else now. A guy. Is that who he came to meet? My heart drops. Does that mean he'll be going soon?

'He's *hot*,' Eliza pronounces. 'Why the hell are you still sitting with *us*?'

I change the subject back to Cassie's work situation, ignoring Eliza's pointed stares and occasional jab beneath the table. But I drink quickly. Because I want to go back to the bar? Or because I need something to cool down my fevered blood?

Only it's not working. My body is vibrating with a sensual need I haven't felt in a long time. Heat is forming between my legs and I am so tempted to do something really stupid. Something I haven't done in a long time.

Of their own accord, and definitely without my permission, my eyes shift towards him. He's propped against the bar with glorious nonchalance, and he's still chatting to the same guy, but his eyes are locked on me. He doesn't try to hide it when I look up.

A thrill of something runs down my spine.

I'm so close to giving in to temptation, and that would be bad. Oh, it would be really good in some ways but…no. *Bad*. Definitely bad.

'Okay, ladies,' I murmur, pushing my almost finished drink aside and standing in one movement. 'I'm going to head home.'

'*What?*' Eliza pulls a face. 'Alone? *Now?* It's so early!'

'I know.' I shrug. 'But if I don't go I think I'll live to regret it.'

I wink at them, so that they can't help but understand my meaning, and then blow each an air-kiss. There's a slight tremble in my legs as I cut my way through the bar. Despite the fact we're past the cut-off for free drinks it's heaving busy now.

My body seems to be in silent rebellion of the decision I've made and is trying to make me change my mind. I don't, though.

When I emerge from the bar's air-conditioned comfort the night's humidity crashes at me like a wave. But it's nothing compared to the fever in my blood. I lift my hand, calling for a taxi, but it sails past.

'Damn it.'

I begin to walk further down the sidewalk, my eyes scanning the street in both directions.

'Hey.'

Though we've only spoken perhaps ten lines of dialogue to one another, his voice is imprinted in my mind. I recognise it instantly, even before I turn around.

'Oh, hey.' My heart is determinedly hammering against my chest.

'You're leaving already?'

When I frown my eyebrows draw together and I get a little line between them. I feel it form now.

'Um… I've left, technically.'

'Right. Where are you headed?'

'Home,' I say firmly, but my body rolls with the potential there. 'Alone.'

It's a defiant stop-sign and he laughs.

'How about one last drink?'

One last drink. With Ethan all-your-dreams-come-true Ash. And then what? I'm already in serious danger of begging him to come home with me. And I suspect he would be incredible in bed. A good lover is one thing, but chemistry can't be faked—and right now the chemistry bubbling between us is practically giving me an orgasm on the spot.

And don't I want that?

Don't I *deserve* that?

There's been no one since Jeremy and I ache for what I think Ethan Ash could do to me. But then what? Am I really ready? How do you know when you are?

I shake my head slowly, not quite meeting his eyes. 'I think that would be a bad idea.' The words are thick, as though my mouth is coated in honey.

'Go on. Live dangerously.'

His wink is the last word in delicious desire.

'*Are* you dangerous?' I ask.

'I think I could be around you.'

There are cars zipping past and people moving quickly around us, and yet it is just him and me, and the air around us seems to throb with awareness and the heaviness of need.

A shiver runs down my spine, but it's not a shiver of darkness or danger so much as one of anticipation. *Oh, God. I'm done for.*

'Isn't that a good reason to stay away?' I say. My brain makes a valiant last-ditch effort to keep my decision in place.

'Depends.'

He moves infinitesimally closer and I breathe in deeply, tasting his masculine fragrance and letting it roll through my blood.

'On what?'

And then he does it again. Just the lightest touch on the back of my hand, but for longer this time, so that I have time to register the contact and enjoy the sensation of desire that resonates through my body.

'On whether you like to live dangerously.'

'Not generally,' I respond quickly, my lips flicking with a tight smile.

'That surprises me.'

'Why? You don't know anything about me.'

He drops his hand away. The absence of touch leaves me feeling bereft.

'Don't I?'

'How could you? We just met.'

'Mmm…'

God, just that single throaty sound of acknowledgement sends a riot tumbling through my veins.

'I know you have the most beautiful hair I've ever seen.'

I've heard that line before. Why do men feel the need to compliment hair? Mine is striking more than beautiful, but I've long ago given up feeling self-conscious about the thick rust-coloured mane that was the bane of my middle school existence, when my white skin, freckled nose and fire-engine-red hair led to almost daily teasing.

Yes, I've heard the line before, but it's never made my stomach flip like this. I've never *believed* the line.

Thanks to the pioneering efforts of Christina Hendricks, right around the time I was hitting college, I made a kind of peace with my peaches and cream complexion, voluptuous figure and rusty hair, but I still never bought the pick-up lines. The guys who told me they loved my curves and dimples.

How easy it is to ignore flattery! But there's something in his eyes, his face and his voice that renders me incapable of being dismissive now.

'I know that your eyes show me everything you're feeling and that your skin is like salt-water pearls.'

My laugh is a hoarse sound in the swirling atmosphere of need. 'That's all *very* cheesy.'

It's not. It's really not. Maybe it's the fact he writes and sings some of the most famous love songs of all time, but he can totally pull this off. This guy, and this guy alone, can make those lines sound like they're being spoken for the first time ever.

His laugh answers mine, and I'm smiling even as I want to acquiesce to his flirtation and do as he bids—live dangerously.

'Even if it's true?'

My breath catches in my throat and I look away—straight into the curious eyes of a woman a few feet away. She's studying us and her cell phone is in her hand.

Strange how quickly I have forgotten that Ethan

Ash is a celebrity. Heat spreads through my cheeks and he follows my gaze, quickly assessing the reason for it. Now he touches me with more urgency, placing a hand in the small of my back and leading me further down the street.

'So?'

'So what?'

I toss a look over my shoulder. The woman is still there, cell phone still in hand. Busybody! I guess this is par for the course for him, but I can't imagine that. Being watched and observed all the time. Having people think they have a right to pry into your life, crack the lid off it whenever it suits them. *No thanks.*

'Want to take a walk on the wild side?'

'I…' My footing stumbles a little as my eyes skid to his and all sense of gravity and order tips off balance. 'I'm not sure.'

I look away.

'How about we start with your name and you can make your mind up over a quiet drink?'

'I…'

I'm struck dumb. I don't think that's ever happened to me in my whole life. Acknowledging that brings a smile to my face.

'I think I'd like that.'

His smile shines bright light and heat into every microscopic corner of my world.

'Then let's get going.'

CHAPTER TWO

WE'RE SHEPHERDED INTO the obviously incredibly exclusive bar with a degree of fanfare that might make even the Queen of England envious. At the bar around the corner from our flat, with its neon lights and pumping songs, it was easy to miss the degree of Ethan Ash's celebrity. Not to ignore the fact that he's unique and different and special, but that these are qualities he has independent of his fame.

Here the deference is marked and reverent, his celebrity obvious and noteworthy. He is treated like the Second Coming, and some of that glory deflects nicely on to me, as his obvious companion.

And it *is* obvious. He kept his hand in the small of my back the whole way here, and he stays close by me as we weave our way through the establishment. I like him being close.

Close enough that I can smell his fragrance and enjoy his warmth.

Close enough that I can slip into the fantasy of what it would be like—*will* be like?—to touch his body all over. To kiss him. To taste him.

I stifle a groan, dipping my head forward to hide the liquid desire that is taking over my body. Desire is unexpected and yet it is welcome. After Jeremy I wasn't sure I'd ever feel it again.

'Here?'

He nods towards a cosy booth seat and every cell in my body ratchets up with awareness. Of him, of me, of the intimacy of that booth.

I nod slowly, then slide in ahead of him. 'Do you come here often?'

He shakes his head. 'Nah, not really my scene.'

'That's interesting. It's very much *my* scene.' I wink at him. 'At least more so than the place we were in before.'

'Yeah, you were a bit of a fish out of water there.'

'Really?' I wrinkle my nose. 'Why do you say that?'

He shrugs. 'Gin and tonic?'

It takes me a second to realise he's asking me a question—what kind of drink I want. A second longer to realise that he knows my regular drink.

'How did you…?'

'You ordered it right in front of me.'

'I also ordered a Prosecco and a vodka gimlet.'

'But you gave those to your friends.'

The certainty that he's been watching me oozes pleasure over my skin. I think he knows, because his smile hints at the same kind of pleasure reverberating inside him. Heat is a burst between us.

'So I did.' I lean forward conspiratorially. 'You're not some kind of stalker, are you?'

His laugh is heaven. 'Not until the last hour or so.'

More pleasure. His compliments are doing everything they should, and even though I'd like to think I'm genuinely hard to impress—thank you, Jeremy—I feel myself soften towards him.

Curiosity is as rampant in my body as desire. 'So,' I say, leaning in closer towards him. 'What's your name?'

For a second I have him fooled. Surprise etches across his face and then he bursts out laughing.

'What?' I continue the charade, my eyes wide, expression droll. 'Why is that funny?'

He sobers. 'It's not.' He clears his throat. 'I'm… Christopher Smith.'

A smile tickles my lips. 'Pleased to meet you, Christopher Smith.'

I wonder how often Ethan Ash gets hit on by girls who are more drawn in by his rock god status than anything else? I wonder if that makes him cynical about women? Or if it makes him think he's God's gift? In my case, I'm definitely not doing anything to disabuse him of that notion. In fact I seriously suspect that if God *did* gift women a man purely for pleasure it would be this guy.

But, hang on. He's hot, sure, and he has the voice of a husky alpha-angel—but he could be *awful* in bed, right?

The thought brings a frown to my face. Isn't there some rule of thumb about that? The really gorgeous guys don't have to work for it so they never learn to be good? Am I going to test that theory with Ethan one-look-will-melt-your-panties-off Ash?

I shift a little in the seat. Our knees brush beneath the table and I suck in a sharp breath. Apparently I am.

He catches the involuntary gesture and his smile is sensual. 'You're nervous?'

I don't know if I'm nervous or surprised. This juggernaut has picked me up and it's dragging me along with it, and I feel a strange disconnect with my own autonomy. 'Maybe.'

He lifts a hand in the air without taking his attention from my face. 'Because of me?'

I shake my head, biting down on my lip. His eyes roam my face like it's a continent he must conquer. He sees everything.

The sense of familiarity is as overwhelming as it is bizarre. I'm sitting in a booth with a bona fide rock star. I should feel strange, but I don't. It all feels so *right*.

'What's your name?'

'Ally.'

'Ally.'

He rolls it around his mouth as if tasting the two symbols. His accent is even hotter when he's saying my name. He makes the A sound like a sigh…'Ah'.

'Is that short for something?'

I nod.

'Gonna make me guess?'

I grin, and my eyes lift as a waitress approaches,

her pale blonde hair pulled into a braid that wraps around her head like a crown.

'Good evening. Here are some menus.' She places two dark books on the tabletop. 'Can I get you a drink to start?'

Ethan turns away to address the waitress. He orders a beer and a gin and tonic, then adds some onion rings for good measure. In profile, he's fascinating. I hadn't noticed until then the bump halfway down his nose that speaks, presumably, of it having been broken at some point in his life. In an accident? Or a fight?

Goosebumps dance down my spine as I imagine the rather sexy image of Ethan Ash in a fist-fight with someone. He'd be a good fighter. Not prone to aggression, I'd bet, but definitely able to take care of himself.

Wow. I didn't even know that I found that kind of thing attractive.

'Alexandra?' he says as he spins back to me.

I don't instantly understand what he's saying, and then I realise. He's guessing my full name.

'No.'

'Hmm…' A low, gruff growl.

Help me, Jesus, I am about to sin.

Beneath the table his fingers find my knee and he strums it like a guitar, gently lashing his fingers over my flesh so that my breath is raspy.

'Do I get a penalty?'

'Definitely.'

'And what would that be?'

I tilt my head to the side, my eyes dancing with amusement even as desire makes my lids heavy.

'Every time you get it wrong,' I say, after a long beat of silence has stretched between us, 'I get to ask you anything I want.'

He lifts his brows skyward. 'Sure. Sounds fair. So, what do you want to know?'

Great question. What *do* I want to know? 'How does *everything* sound?'

He laughs. '"Everything" could take a while. There's twenty-eight years to cover.'

'Let's start with what brings you to the Big Old Apple?'

'A gig. And recording.'

'An album?'

He shakes his head and leans closer, so that his words whisper gently across my cheek.

'That's a separate question.'

'No fair!'

I lift a hand to playfully push at his chest, except the moment my fingers connect with his warm strength no pushing occurs. I hold my hand against him, my eyes meet his, and I feel like I'm sinking hard and fast, with no hope of saving myself.

'Alita?'

I shake my head and dredge up a smile, but it feels heavy on my face because it has to wade through all the desire that's chewing my insides up.

'You're recording an album?'

'Sorta.'

'What does "sorta" mean?'

He shifts his body a little, bringing himself closer to me. 'I'm tinkering. Sketching.'

'Sketching?'

'You know… Getting a feel for some new stuff. Working on pieces.'

'You do that in a recording studio?'

'Sometimes.' He shrugs.

My hand feels the ripple of his muscles and my gut clenches correspondingly.

'And you snuck an extra question in there. Don't think I didn't notice.'

'Uh-huh. I'm very sneaky.'

'I like sneaky.'

His head dips closer. My breath is burning through me.

'Alena?'

When I shake my head this time it brings me closer. Our lips are barely an inch apart and my hand is still on his chest, my fingertips teasing the soft fabric of his shirt. Up close, his scent is intoxicating.

'What's your question?'

My brain is thick and woolly. I want to kiss him. I want to kiss him so badly that I can phantom-feel his lips on mine already.

What if he's a terrible kisser?

My eyes drop to his lips, assessing the possibility of that.

No.

He won't be.

I'm sure of it.

'Don't have one, huh?' he teases.

A noise cracks us apart. I blink, like I'm waking from a dream. The waitress has placed our drinks on the tabletop and then a basket of onion rings. It's surprisingly sweet that he ordered something so pedestrian. Had I expected he'd ask for caviar-dressed lobster?

'What's it like? Being famous?'

His expression shows surprise. He wasn't expecting that.

'You're the first person to ask me that,' he muses, drawing the foam top off his beer in a way that is so absolutely masculine my knees knock with feminine heat.

'Really?' I sound normal. That's good. 'You weren't born famous. It must be a bit weird.'

'Weird's a good word for it.' He shrugs. 'I don't notice so much now. But at first…'

'You were…how old? When your first record came out?'

'I didn't release a record at first. I was big on YouTube before any of the labels came knocking.'

'So you've been doing this a really long time?'

He reaches for an onion ring, crunches it. 'I was sixteen when I topped the UK charts.'

I'm impressed—obviously. All the more so because he says it without a hint of arrogance. It's just a fact, one he's accepted as a part of the fabric of his story, so that he says it without realising what a huge deal it is.

'Do you like it?'

'Music?'

'Fame,' I correct, sipping my drink.

'Nah. It's shit.'

I laugh—it's not what I was expecting him to say at all. 'Really?'

'Really.' He grins. 'You get used to it, but at first it's like being on a different planet. I'll never forget the first time I opened my front door to a throng of paparazzi. It was madness. I was still living at home—we had to move to a gated community with security fences and cameras. I can't get over how fascinated people are by the minutiae of my life. Of anyone else's life. I once had a busboy sell the cutlery I'd used for lunch on eBay.'

I pull a face, barely able to imagine the invasiveness of that.

'But the music…'

He grins and my heart flops.

'I live for it, you know? Always have.'

And he begins to hum, something low and deep, and he moves closer to me again, propping an elbow on the table to form a sort of cage around me. He is big and I'm not. I've always been little, but in the circle created by his arms I feel something I've never felt before. I feel safe.

Safe?

From what?

It's a stupid, errant thought. After all, whatever's happening between us is possibly the most danger I've been in. Even with the guys I was with before Jeremy it was never like this. I was in control. Always.

Ethan when-is-he-going-to-kiss-me? Ash is definitely *not* eating out of the palm of my hands. *Yet.*

A need to grasp control out of his hands spins through me. I reach up and curl my fingers around his shirt, so that I can pull him closer still, and then I brush my lips to his so that I feel the notes rather than just hear them. If possible, his voice tastes even better than it sounds.

'Alison?' he says against my lips.

I shake my head.

'Do you have a question for me?'

I'm at a crossroad. Past, future and present swirl around me. Need, want, right and wrong. These are all voices and forces throbbing in my head. But one voice is loudest of all.

Desire shouts through me.

'Can we go yet?'

Every time I question the wisdom of this I think of the freaking Tweet. *#soinlove*

Sienna's moved on. Why the hell shouldn't I have some fun too?

Something squeezes inside me and my past with Sienna flashes before me. The years we spent together. The way we came through the industry together. I get her and she gets me. It damned near killed me when we broke up. Only her promise that it was temporary eased that pain.

And now she's fucking engaged to another guy.

A new sense of urgency powers my intent.

'Hell, yeah. Let's get out of here.'

I drain my beer, noticing she's hardly touched her drink. I nod towards it but she shakes her head.

'I'm okay.'

She's better than okay. Briefly I feel a wave of guilt. To Sienna. To Ally. There's no doubt in my mind that I'm not thinking one hundred percent clearly, but my instincts are telling me to go with this—or is that my cock?—and I'm not going to ignore them.

'Let's go.'

I hold my hand out and she places her palm in mind. Her hand's small, and yet it fits into mine perfectly. I stand and pull her closer to me as I do. She smells like vanilla and moonlight.

Someone's tipped the press off as to my whereabouts, so that when we step out of the club there's flashes everywhere. Ally's surprised. She's not used to fame and its pointed intrusion. I pull her closer to my chest. The desire to protect her is instinctive. I don't want her being collateral damage in all of this.

I hail a cab and it stops instantly. I hold the door open for her and she slips inside, a blur of pale skin, bright blue eyes and long red hair. I follow, moving close to her in the back of the cab.

I hear every single one of Ally's rushed breaths echo inside my soul.

I give the driver my hotel address and then I turn to Ally. I don't know what I'm going to say to her. Thoughts fly from my head at the sight of her huge wide eyes and parted lips.

Fuck it.

I want her.

I kiss her as though my life depends on it. I kiss her with an aching hunger and desperation that surprises us both.

Or maybe it doesn't—because it's exactly how she kisses me back.

CHAPTER THREE

IS IT POSSIBLE to pass out from pleasure? I know that's generally the body's response to painful stimuli, but is it possible to be so turned on that the pleasure almost becomes pain? I've never had sex in a cab, but if this drive takes any longer I'm going to do just that.

His hand is on my thigh and his tongue is tangled with mine, his lips move over mine and I am melting into the leather of the seat. Desire is like a volcano in my core, bursting with lava-like heat. He runs his fingers higher, confidently, firmly, until he reaches the lace of my thong. He pads his fingertips across me there and I groan into his mouth, my fingers lifting to knot into his thick hair, my body weak and strong all at once.

He removes his hand from between my legs and his desertion is a wave that flushes me with ice. I grind my hips impatiently and make a whimpering sound as his flat palm drags up my body, over the softness of my clothes to the curves of my breast. He rolls his hand across me as though I am an ob-

ject and he its owner. His touch sends spirals of fire
deep into my body, affecting me on a cellular level.

I make a gurgling sound and laugh, pushing up
to kiss him harder, to let my breasts flatten his hand
between us. We are wedged together and my hands
are curled around his neck and, God, he tastes and
feels amazing. Better than amazing.

Finally the cab pulls to a stop and I am flushed
with relief—until I realise it's a stop sign.

'You've gotta be fucking kidding me,' he snaps,
his brow furrowed as he shoots an impatient look
through the glass of his windscreen.

He feels it too, then. This need that is reverberating through the back of the cab somewhere in the
middle of Park Avenue. It makes me feel inexplicably relieved, knowing that I'm not the only one out
here on this limb.

He turns to look at me and I laugh at the bewil-
derment on his features.

'I swear to God, if this takes much longer...'

I totally get it. Hadn't I just been thinking the
same thing?

I swallow, trying to bring moisture back into my
parched mouth. My hand is still on his chest; I can
feel the rapid beating of his heart. *Thump, thump,
thump.*

Craning my head around, I can just make out the
street sign that shows we're on the corner of Park
Avenue and East Twenty-Second. 'You said the
Gramercy?'

'Yeah.'

'It's like a block away. Let's walk.'

He arches a brow, and heat simmers through me as he reaches forward and taps on the glass.

'We'll get out here.'

He tosses some money through the window and winks at me, opening the door and stepping out so that he can hold it wide for me. I follow, my foot landing on the pavement for the briefest moment before his arm wraps around my waist and draws me to him.

I don't think the cab has even driven off before his lips are back on mine, with renewed intensity and urgency. His body is strong and he pushes me easily, guiding me to the sandstone wall of some building. It's cold and hard behind me, and he's hard and hot against me, his body all angles and planes and thick strong legs surrounding me, holding me still as he grinds against me. His arms are my cage and, *oh*, the sweetness of being trapped by him!

His mouth holds my head to the wall and I devour him as he devours me, my hands curling around his back to find the waistband of his jeans. I slide my fingers beneath his shirt, groaning as warm skin rewards my seeking. It's so soft and smooth beneath me. I draw my fingertips on a slow exploration higher, along the ridges of his spine and then to his sides, to hips that are carved and firm.

'Fuuuuck...'

He groans into my mouth, wrenching his head away—and it is a wrench. Every line of his body speaks to that. It is as though he's had to fight his way through quicksand just to find space between us.

Maybe it's the whole rock star thing. Maybe it makes him sexier than mortals. I don't know. This is so not normal, though. Is it for him?

'I need to get you to my hotel. *Now.*'

I nod, not even bothering to argue with him. But there's a frown between his eyes, just like I always get.

I lift my finger to it, absentmindedly exploring the groove. 'What's wrong?'

The line deepens. He has a dimple in his cheek and when he frowns it's deliciously seductive.

'Nothing. I…' And then he shakes his head, steps back, reaches for my hand.

We've just been simulating sex with our clothes on, and yet there is something bizarrely intimate about the simple act of lacing our fingers together. His, mine, his, mine, his, mine—in and out, they are woven together, and it's a new kind of coming together.

'Let's go.'

I nod, not sure I'm capable of speech anyway.

After a few paces he looks at me with an almost embarrassed grin. 'You look like you've been thoroughly felt up.'

'Felt up?' I laugh. 'I guess I have been, now that you mention it.'

He squeezes my hand and I lift my other hand to run it over my hair. Always difficult to contain, it is beyond wild now. His fingers have done that. The knowledge makes my tummy flip.

'Sooo…' he says on a laugh. A husky laugh. 'This isn't how I thought my night would be going down.'

I don't know if it's an intentional *double entendre* but I have an instant image of him doing just that—going down on me—in my mind, and my face heats up.

Unknowingly, I quicken my step. 'You and me both,' I hear myself respond, hugely impressed at my ability to sound almost normal.

'What were your plans tonight?'

'Drinks with the girls.' I shrug. 'Then home by ten to catch up on *Poldark* and do a face mask.'

He pulls a face.

'What? You don't approve?'

'Of *Poldark*? It's something my mother watches.'

'Mmm… Her and every other red-blooded woman on the planet.'

'Seriously?'

He squeezes my hand again. I love the way that feels. Like he's reaching right into my heart and giving it a little paddle with electricity.

'Uh, *yeah*. *Poldark* is awesome. Hot, hot, *hot*. You should watch it.'

'After that recommendation? How could I not?'

We stop at an intersection and traffic moves through it, too thick for us to go against the lights. And so we wait.

The night is balmy—I love New York nights like this.

'Yeah. Summer's got something going for it.'

I hadn't realised I'd spoken aloud until he answered my observation. He pulls my hand, so that I bump closer to him. I love the way he smells. The way he feels. A shiver of something a bit like apprehension runs down my spine but I refuse to analyse it. The problem is, though, I'm really not *this* girl any more. I used to be able to just roll with the night... have fun without taking a second to think about the consequences.

When, exactly, did I grow out of that?

I remember learning to drive and my dad telling me that young people always think they're invincible. I guess it's true. It's so easy to believe that nothing will happen—nothing will go wrong.

And nothing *has* gone wrong for me, yet caution has set into my bones along with age. At twenty-five I am less able to ignore the paths before me, and I wonder which this night will lead to.

After we've slept together—then what? Do I stay the night? Or creep out while he sleeps? If I stay, do we have breakfast together?

And then...?

Do I give him my number and wonder if Ethan I-have-won-a-million-Grammys Ash will call me? Worse, do I take *his* number and then call him? Agonising over what to say and whether he wants to see me again?

'So, Alesandre, when you're not being impossibly sexy in tacky bars what do you do with yourself?'

'Alesandre is just the Italian version of Alexandra, you know.'

'Mmm. So that's a no. Altona?'

I laugh and shake my head. The lights switch to green and we move across the street, each as swiftly as the other, our mutual anxiety to be in privacy barrelling towards us.

'My flatmates chose the venue.' I wrinkle my nose. 'They like it.'

They like the prices, really, but loyalty keeps me quiet on that score. Cassie's a Broadway actress, but roles are few and far between and she's forever auditioning and waiting for her big break. She's an incredible performer, though—I have no doubt she'll hit it big. Eliza is a primary school teacher, and while she works hard she seems to spend almost her entire salary on stuff for her students. New supplies, craft projects, science experiments...

Maybe if she didn't insist on doing that we'd be able to drink in slightly more salubrious accommodations.

'You're not from New York?'

'How can you tell?' I look up at him, surprise obvious on my face.

He draws us to a slow stop just before moving down East Twenty-Second. 'Your accent.'

'You can pick up on that?'

He grins. 'Is that weird?'

I bite down on my lip to stop myself groaning at how damned sexy the twist of his lips is. Ahead of us, the retro light installation above the Gramercy Park Hotel leads a path to our immediate future. Beneath it there's a huddle of people. I'm not sure, at first, why they're just standing there—and then I make out the shape of a long-lens camera.

'There's paparazzi at your hotel.' My eyes lift to his face.

A muscle throbs against his jaw, like he's clenching his teeth or thinking dark thoughts. My insides clench.

'You go ahead of me,' he says.

'Will that work?'

He looks at me for a long moment and then nods. 'Yeah. Wait for me at the lifts inside.'

It's easy enough for me to slip past the paparazzi. One photographer lifts his camera and holds it poised at my face. But then, when he sees through the lens that I am nobody, he drops it once more.

I am glad I am nobody.

I am glad I am not *her*.

The woman who ruined a family.

Guilt sledges through me.

Ethan Ash isn't Jeremy, and this isn't a big deal.

It's just…sex. Fun. Easy. Nothing serious.

Nonetheless, my heart palpitates furiously as I turn and look over my shoulder, catching sight of him as he saunters—yes, *saunters*—across the street, hands in the pockets of his well-worn jeans, head tilted at an angle that shows the hard lines of his face.

Desire whips me.

I move quickly across the foyer, wanting to be well beyond the paparazzi's point of interest by the time Ethan joins me. I catch a brief impression of sumptuous red carpet, black and white tiles, enormous crystal chandeliers, animal skins and a fire that would, in winter, create warmth and cosiness with stunning ease.

The elevators are simply shining doors submerged behind wood panelling. I wait beside them, staring straight ahead. I hear the rush of lenses clicking and buttons being pressed and I don't look. There's the rustle of a doorman moving outside, and then he is beside me, his finger jabbing at the button of the lift with obvious impatience. We don't look at one another.

After only a few seconds, the doors ping open. It's empty.

We step in and Ethan swipes a key card before pressing one of the old-fashioned radio buttons on the panel. It whooshes upwards and my tummy whooshes with it.

I have *never* wanted a guy this badly.

The atmosphere is heavy with that feeling, that need. It practically hums around us, so that it takes every ounce of my willpower not to press the stop button and beg him to fuck me then and there.

I dig my nails into my palms as extra insurance.

The doors ping open—finally—and even as we step out of the lift he's reaching for me. Now, in the privacy of the hotel corridor, he lifts me off the ground, his arms tight around my waist as his mouth moves over mine, and he walks like I weigh nothing, and carrying me is nothing more than a minor inconvenience. His lips are punishing and I am submissive, taking the kiss, begging for more even as my legs lift, needing greater purchase, more intimacy, closeness—everything.

I wrap them around him and groan as I hear the unmistakable tearing of my skirt—which was definitely *not* designed to be spread-eagled around a rock star's waist. *Whoops.* Somewhere in my mind I discover another consequential path of this coming together—some makeshift outfit assembly will be required in order for me to get home, whenever it is I *do* go home.

Without releasing his grip, without lifting his lips, he fumbles the key card against the door. The first time is unsuccessful and he swears into my mouth as the door remains resolutely closed. Second time it springs open and we burst through it. The door slams shut and Ethan drops the key card to the floor like litter, striding deeper into the suite.

I have a brief impression of more luxury, more red, more chandeliers made of beaded crystal—and an enormous bed that is like an oasis in the midst of a never-ending desert. But he turns sharply, propping me against a table instead.

The second my butt connects with the tabletop his hands reach for my blouse and he pulls at it, ripping every single button so that they pop and fly across the room like angry little witnesses to my thwarted needs.

It's a damned nice blouse—one of my favourites—but I don't bemoan its demise. I am as eager as he is to be naked and touching all over. I arch my back as he pushes the fabric down my arms, his fin-

gers tracing my flesh as he frees me of the garment
before they lift higher, finding my bra. He traces a
thumb over the lace and I swear I whimper as though
I'm about to come. I think I *am* about to come.

My eyes skittle to his face, shock in all my features. He understands. I know he does. He curves
his hands around my butt and drags me to the edge
of the table, so that I can feel the hard, aching heat of
his cock through the fabric of his jeans, straining at
it, practically breaking it. My fingers seek it—seek
him. They fumble at his button and then a noise of
triumph erupts from my lips as I find the zip and
push it downwards.

But he's moving, pushing at my bra, freeing my
breasts in one moment and claiming them with his
mouth the next. His tongue lashes my nipple as his
fingers roll the other, and his dick grinds against me
through the fabric of our clothes.

Perspiration sheens my skin. I lift my fingers from
his jeans, from their futile mission of cock-hunting,
and curl them around his hips instead, digging my
nails into him, lifting my feet to the edges of the table
and crying out as his teeth press into my nipple with
enough pressure to make me see stars.

I'm at the edge of the world. Ethan's there too, but
I'm the one who's stepping off…who's being flung
off! I dig my nails in harder and he rolls his mouth to
my other breast, bringing his fingers to tease where
his teeth have just been. It's too much. The sensations and juxtapositions. The heat of his mouth and

the coldness of the air-conditioned hotel room. The softness of his fingertips and the hurt of his teeth.

I cry out loudly as an orgasm crashes over me, sucking me under, rendering me the opposite of mute. I am loud and I am desperate and I have no grasp of control. No grasp of time, space or date either, to be honest. If you'd asked me where I was, I would have needed a shot of black coffee to wake up and remember.

I am doused in more sensations than I was even aware existed and yet I'm not done. *He's* not done. This is just the beginning.

'I want to fuck you.'

'Isn't that what you're doing?' I smile up at him, my body singing.

'Hell, yeah.'

He pulls at my butt, jerking me closer to him, and then he rolls his cock against me so that I cry out again.

'Please, Ethan…' I groan hungrily.

Apparently he doesn't need to be asked twice. He reaches into his pocket and pulls out his wallet, then slides a condom from within its folds.

There is a small part of me that is consciously cheering what is about to happen—unlike my body, which is so in the moment. This isn't just sex. It isn't just relief. It's release—it's an exorcism. I am going to fuck another man, and with every moment and motion I am going to blot Jeremy further from my mind.

I am going to reduce his importance in my life.

With sex.

'I've never been happier to see a little foil square.' I grin, reaching for it. 'Now. Let me see what I'm dealing with here.'

His grin is like warm treacle on a hot day. 'You're mighty impatient... Alicia.'

Hearing him say my real name is the biggest turn-on yet. And that's saying something.

My eyes meet his and he knows.

'Alicia.'

Even better than Ally. My name tastes wonderful on his mouth. He pushes at his jeans and I take over, sliding my hands into his grey cotton boxers, feeling the curve of his ass—of course it's a fantastic ass. I hold his eyes as I bring my hands to the front, feeling for his long, hard dick. As I enclose it in my fist, wrapping my hand around it hungrily, he lets out a hoarse groan.

'How do you feel about being fucked fast?'

His laugh is borderline apologetic, and there's a vulnerability that makes me ache for more than just this. But only for a moment.

'I feel really, really good about that.'

I rip the top off the condom with my teeth and then slide it over him as he steps out of his jeans. For a moment I wonder at his size—I haven't slept with anyone in a really long time. Is it possible I've forgotten that dicks do this when they're hard? But it's big. Really big. And beautiful.

A shiver swirls through me. He pushes his shirt off impatiently and then he's lifting me up once more, carrying me against his chest, cradling me, into the bedroom. He throws me on the bed and reaches for the remains of my skirt, tearing it off me and then pulling my thong down my legs.

It's not slow, like he was with the bra. His hands graze my legs, my calves, my thighs, but that's accidental. He needs me now as much as I need him. There's no sense denying it. No sense in pretending.

As he brings himself over me I push my palm against his chest, knocking him so that he is on his side, next to me, and we're face to face. I kiss him as I hitch my leg over his hip, and then push up on my knee so that I'm straddling him.

I don't know why having control is important to me, but I suppose if I had to analyse it I would probably say that I feel so utterly out of my depth in what I'm feeling that I need *something* to make me have a sense of agency.

Choice is my agency, though, and I choose *this*. I choose to move on. I choose to forget. I choose not to let Jeremy make me cower any more. I choose all of what we're doing.

And my choice has nothing to do with anything other than desire and need and everything to do with Ethan Ash and me—Alicia Douglas.

We are two chemicals, mixing together, swirling, swarming and about to explode.

'Fuck me,' I whisper as I lift up and lower myself over him, taking his length deep inside me slowly, letting my muscles adjust to this strange newness. To his size and his needs.

I almost can't bear the perfection of that moment. The haunting rightness.

He lets out a long, slow grunt and his fingers dig into my hips. He holds me down, low on his length, and he throbs, pulses. I feel every jerk of his desire deep inside me. I hold my breath, chewing on my lip as my nerve-endings quiver in response. His cock is whispering secrets within me and my body is listening intently.

It's but a moment. A magical moment. And then he's moving, holding my hips low as he thrusts, his abs rippling with each movement. I drop lower, my mouth chasing each ridge of his chest, my tongue flicking his hair-roughened nipples, my body pressed against his.

His fingers roam my flesh again, like an object, like he owns me, and I love the feeling of being owned by him. I roll my hips and he swears, moving his hands to hold my face, dragging me up to his mouth, to kiss me. And he pushes up, flipping me onto my back while barely breaking the kiss.

Oh, God. It's bone-meltingly perfect. Like this, he is deep, so deep, and he thrusts harder and faster and his tongue echoes the movements. I lift my legs and his hands grab my ankles, pushing them higher, moving them over his shoulders so that he has complete access to me. It breaks the kiss but I don't care, because now his lips are moving over my leg, and every thrust is waving me on, nearer to explosive release.

I dig my fingers into his shoulders and there it is!

I cry out as the orgasm shreds me, my hand lifting to his chest to still him, to implore him to wait, so that I am able to feel every tremor of the earthquake he's created. He knows. He waits. He is patient. The only sound in the room is that of his breathing, loud and hoarse, his control almost at breaking point. But he watches me, watches the effect of pleasure on my face, my skin, and then, when he knows— because he *knows* me—that I can take it again, he moves once more, slowly at first, letting new sensations build up, before he drops my legs back to the bed and brings his mouth to my mouth, kissing me, making me groan under the weight of the rightness of that moment.

The next time I come it's with him. We are both on the edge of the cliff, stepping off it together. My fingers seek his and I lace them together again, and that act of intimacy means everything and nothing as our bodies sing in unison.

We are entwined. Him, me, and the luxury of the Park View Suite. I fear that I am lost. Or is that I'm found?

CHAPTER FOUR

IN AND OUT. In and out. I breathe slowly, trying to calm my racing pulse, my raging nervous system, but still my body is part electrical current, part hurricane.

'Okay,' I murmur softly, more to myself than anything else. I'm processing it. Or trying to.

What just happened?

He pushes up onto one elbow so that he can look down into my eyes and I spy the galaxy in his.

'Okay.' He grins. 'That was...'

'Perfect,' I supply, lazily tracing a drop of sweat as it runs down his chest. He leans forward to kiss my fingertip and his dick, still strong inside me, makes me groan anew.

So far as exorcisms go, I think we might have nailed it.

'Yeah.' He nods. 'It was.'

He kisses me again, but this time it's slow. Gentle. A kiss of curiosity that I welcome. *Damn it*. I'm back at those paths, looking at each of them, wondering, wondering, and uncertainty is making my knees weak.

Do I want his curiosity? Do I welcome it? Or does it speak too strongly of wanting other things than this bed, this man, this night?

'Are you hungry?'

'Hungry?' I blink, the question not at all what I expected.

He nods against my lips, then braces his forehead against mine. 'Yeah. You know, that thing people get? It generally involves needing food. Eating. Maybe conversation.'

'I'm familiar with the concept.'

My own little divot forges between my brows and his eyes lift to it. His grins, and that makes me smile, erasing the similarity.

He rolls his hips luxuriantly, slowly throbbing warmth through me, and desire surges like a wave at high tide, rolling inwards towards the shore. I lift my hips to meet it, to welcome it.

'Room Service,' he murmurs. 'Definitely Room Service.'

Still inside me, he stretches, reaching for the phone on the bedside table, and my whole body stretches with his, reluctant to relinquish even a hint of connection.

He brings his mouth back to mine, the phone hooked casually under one ear.

'Ethan Ash,' he says, and my eyes lift to his, surprised until I realise he's speaking to someone else.

That surprise, though, is nothing compared to

what shoots through me when he pulls out of me, leaving me instantly bereft, before inserting a finger deep into my core. I can't help the moan that escapes my mouth. It falls out like a waterfall, slumberous and urgent at the same time.

His finger swirls around already-over-sensitised nerve-endings and I arch my back as he brings his mouth to my breast at the same time.

'Two crab linguine. Some fruit.'

'A peach,' I whisper.

'A peach,' he repeats, then drags his mouth across my chest, his stubbled jaw making the raw, aching, sensitive flesh tremble beneath him.

His mouth is an instant relief. And as he rolls my nipple with his tongue he speaks into the phone. The words are husky against me. I feel his voice a baritone on my skin. And he feels me inside.feels my heart and my core.

'Definitely champagne. Lots of champagne.' He draws his lips lower, to my navel, and then, still with the phone under his chin, to my clit.

'Oh, my God!' I squawk as his tongue finds the cluster of nerves and flicks it punishingly.

'Ice cream,' he adds, his fingers curling around my ankles and pushing my legs apart on the bed.

There is a tiny part of me that is embarrassed by this intimacy—but only a tiny part. The rest of me is way up on cloud nine, wondering if any woman has ever felt this good. If any person has ever known this pleasure.

I presume he's done ordering, because he drops

the phone to the ground. The cord is still stretched across the bed but I don't ask him to hang up. Nor do I attempt to do so. I'm not moving, and I'm not going to encourage him to do anything that might bring an end to this sweet, sensual invasion.

'A peach, huh?' he murmurs against me.

I dig my nails into the bed, trying to breathe, trying not to fall apart.

'Yeah.'

'A favourite?'

'Mmm, yes…' I don't think I'm talking about fruit any more.

'You taste fucking amazing.'

Even that doesn't embarrass me. I groan in response, reaching above me for a pillow, which I drag down, holding it over my face as I cry out and he continues to run his tongue over me with the kind of skill that should win him a gold medal. Seriously. If oral sex were a competitive sport then this guy could hang up his microphone. He's *that* good.

His hands lift up, finding my breasts, and he knows what I love already. He's learned fast. He tweaks my nipples and palms the roundness of my flesh, and his mouth lifts me up and carries me away until I can stand it no longer, and I give in to the euphoric relief that has been building and bursting.

I feel it drop over me and whimper into the pillow. Which is no help, actually, because it smells intoxicatingly like him. So like him that I want to take it with me. *Uh-oh.* Another road opens up before me. I resolutely shut all paths out and surrender to the sensations of *this*. This very, very, *very* delightful everything.

He slows down as he feels me come apart, still touching me, tasting me, but no longer driving me to insane heights. I have exploded and now I am recovering. I am trying to catch my breath. He stays close and I'm comforted by his closeness—until he pulls back and stands in one fluid moment.

He's still wearing the condom—but not for long. He rolls it off and wraps it in a tissue, tossing it carelessly into a wastepaper basket before reaching for the phone and replacing it on the cradle. Then, hands on hips, gloriously naked, he stares down at me, where I'm hiding behind an organic Italian cotton pillow.

'Alicia?'

I can't speak. Maybe not ever again. It is quite possible that he's erased my voice, like some kind of kinky *Little Mermaid* scenario.

'Come here.'

I can't speak, but I can move, and I *will* move as he demands because he's offering me a whole new world of pleasure and I am anxious to enjoy it, and with it to erase Jeremy's significance in my life.

I stand. My legs shake and my skin is raw—pale pink, I see, as I look down at my breasts. The sight of his marks on my body makes me soar. An ancient feminine power rocks me to the core. *He* did this to me. His passion did it to both of us. And the passion was bigger than either of us could control.

'You never answered my question.'

'What question?'

He links his fingers through mine and pulls me gently away from the bed. For the first moment since entering the suite I notice the view.

'Holy shit.' I stand completely still—naked, uncaring. 'Wow…'

Manhattan glistens before me. It is high-rises and high dreams, lights and lives, lows and loves.

'Yeah.'

His voice is hoarse and it draws my attention. I stare at his profile again, and it's so different now. I see all his lines and marks and strengths, and somehow I feel that I know him so much better than even an hour ago.

'I've always loved the contradictions of New York,' I say.

I am drawn to the view and step towards the window, relinquishing his hand without realising it. I press my palm to the glass. It is darkly tinted and I am confident in the privacy it affords.

'So much beauty…so much despair.' My smile is crooked as our eyes latch on to each other in the reflection. 'Nowhere in the world can you find such wealth and poverty in the same city block.'

'It's a unique place,' he agrees. 'Where are you from?'

'Wisconsin, originally. I moved here five years ago—right out of college.'

'What did you study?'

'Fine art and art history.'

I've surprised him. I see the way he nods, but

it's speculative. Funny, because I'm well-known and well-respected in my field, and it's been a long time since I've met anyone who doesn't know what I do.

'You're an artist?'

'I wish…' I sigh wistfully, turning to face him with mock sadness on my face. 'I always wanted to be. My mom says I spent so much time clutching paintbrushes I practically deformed my fingers.'

I lift my hand up and we both stare at it in the silence of the room. They're normal to look at now, but I remember the claw-like grip they manifested after days and days spent hunched at a canvas.

'But…?'

'Can't paint to save my life.' I grimace. 'I'm a buyer now. And an appraiser by appointment.'

'So you take other people's cash to choose fashionable art?'

I shrug. 'Fashionable, abstract, classic. I spend a lot of time with my clients and in the spaces the art will inhabit, making sure it's going to work.'

'That's a *job*?'

'Hell, yeah.' I gesture to the room we're standing in. 'This whole hotel is fitted with contemporary American masterpieces—testaments to the modernist movement. You look around and you see the art and maybe you don't realise the effect it creates. But we're standing in a *movement*, Ethan!'

I hear the enthusiasm and passion in my own voice and wince. I adore my job. That's a good thing, but it can be a bit bizarre to people who don't feel the same way.

'I know what you mean.'

I exhale. 'You do?'

'Well, not exactly…'

He turns and cuts through the suite, disappearing through a door. I follow.

'But the first time I recorded at Abbey Road I just about shit myself. I mean…' He shakes his head as he reaches for the faucet and turns on the water. The bath is around the corner, half hidden by a dark wood-panelled wall. 'The history is thick in the air at that place. The microphones, the carpet, the pictures. Legends—so many, a list as long as my arm. Not just the Beatles—though that's *everything*. But all the bands, musicians, songwriters. It's impossible to explain—except I guess it's like you just said. I was in the middle of something so much bigger than me. It took me three tracks to get the jitters out of my voice.'

'The jitters?'

Oh, no. There goes my heart, flopping just like my tummy has been all night, squeezing with something a lot like affection at the sweetness of that word. *Jitters.* Twenty-eight, sexy as sin, and a gold medallist at pleasure-giving and he uses words like 'jitters'. He gives *me* the jitters.

'Yeah. You know. The heebie-jeebies.'

'Stop.' I burst out laughing and hold a hand up at the same time. 'You need to stop using language like that.'

'Like heebie-jeebies?'

'Yeah. It's too…' *Cute. Adorable. Sweet. Lovely.*

'I'm sorry, Ally, there's no other word for it. I had medically diagnosed heebie-jeebies.'

But he grabs the hand I've held out and pulls it— and me—towards him. Our bodies meld together and his eyes lock to mine. Breath snags in my throat like a piece of thread that won't give. I stare up at him, waiting, transfixed, my heart throbbing.

He kisses my forehead lightly, softly, gently, and a moan is trapped in my throat. *Yes. This. All of this.* The paths are back in my mind, opening up and inviting me to choose one.

There's a sound from outside and he reaches for a towel, breaking the sense of magic that was enveloping me. 'Hop in. I'll join you in a minute.'

'The bath?'

'Why not?'

He wraps a towel around his waist, low-slung so that—if it's possible—he looks even sexier than when he was all gloriously golden and butt-naked.

'You got somewhere else you need to be?'

The paths look at me.

He looks at me.

I expel a long, slow sigh as I shake my head. 'Not right now, I don't.'

'Good. Then you're all mine.' He kisses me quickly on the cheek. 'And I'm going to make the most of it. I'll be right back.'

He disappears from the bathroom but I move to the door and watch him. I watch him because I seem unable to help it. Because I am pulled to him like a bee to honey.

* * *

Her eyes are shut when I step back into the bathroom, bowl in hand. The water swirls around her, and her breasts are two perfect peaks floating on the surface. She's added some of the shower lotion, and the bubbled top creates a frustrating visual barrier to the rest of her body.

A body I now yearn to see again.

To make completely my own.

It is a primal need to possess her, and I'm more surprised by that than I should be. It's been a long time since I've been with a woman. And things between Sienna and me were shit at the end. For a long time *before* the end, actually.

But I don't want to think about her now.

I don't want Sienna in my head, ruining this for me.

'You look good enough to eat.'

Her eyes ping open, searing me with awareness. 'You should know.'

'Uh-huh.'

I grin as I step into the bath, relieved as all fuck when my legs brush against hers. I like touching her. I like it *a lot*.

Maybe it's just the newness of this. The freshness of being with a woman I barely know.

'Definitely something I want seconds of.'

Her cheeks flush bright pink—God, I love how she blushes, and I can't resist teasing her more.

'And thirds…and fourths.'

Darker pink glistens on her cheeks. I settle myself against the head of the bath and scoop some ice cream onto a spoon, holding it out to her. She keeps her eyes locked to mine as she takes a bite. A dribble of vanilla escapes down one side of her chin and I watch its progress. She makes no effort to check it, and after a moment it falls to her décolletage and slips down to where her breast meets the water.

Shit.

She's perfection.

'You know...' I continue, hell-bent now on my mission to make her whole body glow red with knowledge and awareness. 'You make the sweetest noises when you're coming.'

Mission accomplished. She lights up like a Christmas tree, her eyes not meeting mine.

'Why are we eating ice cream?'

It is the most goddamned clunky conversation-change I've ever heard—and I'm often around women who are nervous as all hell.

I laugh, the noise soft in the quietness of the bathroom, and I lift a spoonful of the confection out of the bowl. 'I'll show you.'

I place it in my mouth and then move through the water, finding one of her breasts, which I'm already thinking of as *my* breasts. I know how she loves them to be played with—how much it drives her crazy.

For the smallest moment Sienna is in my head again. And she's pissed off as all hell at what I'm doing.

Anger briefly flares in my gut, followed by satisfaction. I'm glad she's pissed off. She can join the club.

Sienna always was jealous. Jealous of the women who'd get backstage at my concerts. Women the band would introduce me to. Women who'd find out where I was staying and make their way to the hotel and wait outside my room. Women who emailed and Tweeted me their most obscene fantasies in the hopes I'd turn them into lyrics…or reality.

Well, no sense crying over spilled milk or unsown oats. Here, in this enormous bath with Ally, I've got every opportunity to make up for lost time. And I intend to use it.

She's so hot. Like the sex gods recognised my deprivation and decided to reward me with an actual bona fide angel.

I slide the ice cream over her perfect peach nipple, my hands braced on her hips beneath the water so I feel the way she sucks in a hard breath of surprise at the ice-cold invasion. The frozen heat—such a contradiction.

She shifts underwater, dragging her breath lower. I make a 'tsking' sound of disapproval. 'You don't like it?'

'Oh, I like it,' she mutters, without meeting my eyes. 'What I *don't* like is how easily you can drive me crazy. It's not fair.'

'Not fair?' I shake my head. 'Believe me, I get as much out of your pleasure as you do.'

And to prove my point I nudge my dick against

her, so she can feel how hard I am for her already. How no relief could erase the need I feel for her.

'That's reassuring,' she murmurs.

I laugh. 'I'm glad you're reassured, Alicia.'

Something serious flickers in her eyes and she moves forward in the bath, making a small wave that ripples around me and crashes to the edges. She reaches for the ice cream spoon and takes a bite before bringing her mouth to mine. The kiss is hot and cold and I groan into her mouth, my hands seeking first her hair, tangling in its lengths, before dragging themselves down to her hips and squeezing her flesh, loving the feeling of her as she moves over me.

She's so close I want to take her then and there.

Thank God she's still got room for thought. She shakes her head, keeping herself just far enough away from me to inspire a sort of madness. 'No condom,' she murmurs.

I swear, if it hadn't been for that I'd be taking her now, driving into her again.

She kisses me and I move closer and closer to bursting. She rolls her hips against my waist, teasing me, inviting me, even when we both know we can't do this. She's tilting her pelvis, simulating sex, and my temperature is skyrocketing. I'm harder than granite and there's only one cure.

While I want *her*, I want more of this, too. More of feeling like I'm about to explode, like I'm close but far away. I wanted to get blind drunk tonight, but instead I met Ally and I'm drunk on something besides alcohol. Is this just deprivation talking? Just the fact I haven't been able to do this for a really long time?

Flesh on flesh…her under my fingertips.

Fuuuuck.

'What would you say about getting out of the bath?' All I can think about is taking her again. Driving into her like she's my new home.

'Can we bring the ice cream?'

'Hell, *yeah*, we can bring the ice cream.'

She's so graceful. Even as she pushes up to standing and moves out of the bath it's like a ballet performance. She's lithe and lean and, though I'm aching to follow, I take a moment just to watch her. To watch as she pulls her wet hair over her shoulder and squeezes it into a towel, her eyes fixed straight ahead. She drops the towel to her body and pats herself dry in what is my new definition of sexiness. Then she turns back to me and she looks like Mona Lisa might have if she'd just rolled out of bed.

Enigmatic. Hot. Desirable.

'Ready?'

'Yeah.' Is that my voice? So gruff and hoarse?

She reaches for the ice cream and once more spoons it into her mouth, but she holds the spoon there, her eyes holding mine. Just for a second. A beat. But it's enough. Enough for me to imagine it's me in her mouth.

I would be some kind of animal if I didn't feel guilty for what I'm doing. Four months ago I thought Sienna and I would work through our shit and probably one day get married. Four months ago I wouldn't have dreamed of being with someone else.

And now I'm fucking this beautiful, sexy Ally.

Am I doing it to hurt Sienna?

Am I doing it to fuck Sienna right out of my head?

Am I doing it because Sienna deserves that?

Hell, yeah. But I'm also doing it because Ally seems to have robbed me of any ability to walk away. She has drawn me into something I cannot fight.

And I don't want to fight it anyway.

CHAPTER FIVE

THE SUN IS WEAK, straining to break through the sensuality that has formed a deep fog in his room. I squint and stifle a yawn, arching my back until I ram against him. A feline smile curves slowly over my lips. I reach for him on autopilot, turning at the same time as his lips seek mine, crushing against them.

I haven't spent the night in a stranger's bed in a long time, and whenever I have in the past there has been the inevitable dawning of awkwardness the next morning. A raising of self-consciousness along with the new day. A desire to begin the forgetting—forgetting what I've done and with whom.

I do not feel that now.

I lose myself in the kiss and my body seeks his, hungrily, urgently, naturally. He groans into my mouth and it is an answer to my feral needs, my wildness and abandon. For a brief second he is distant, turning away from me, and then I roll with him, straddling him even as he laughs and extends an arm to the side table. He knocks a glass of water to the carpeted floor but doesn't react.

Nor do I. I'm already seeking him, wanting to take him deep inside again. I need him more than I can express.

He laughs. A throaty sound of agreement. And then he swears. 'Hang on.'

I don't want to hang on, yet I pause, just long enough to frown and follow his fumbling hand. *Oh, shit.* A condom—of course. Had I really almost forgotten? Colour flushes my cheeks, but embarrassment is quickly swallowed by something else. Something far more primal.

Even before he's ripped the packet open I'm bending my head forward and my mouth is taking him in the way the rest of me wants to. I curve my lips around him until he reaches the back of my throat and he swears again. I feel the curse reverberate through his body and into mine.

I don't stop.

His fingers push through my hair, tangling in its length, and I move my mouth upwards, then take him all the way in again, over and over.

'Fuuuck.'

He drops his fingers to my shoulders and pushes me up. I stare past his cock, beautiful as it is, up his toned chest, to a face that really is the stuff of dreams. God, he's hot. Seriously hot.

The kind of guy a girl could lose her mind for.

And her heart too?

Not me—not my heart. My heart is staying boxed in my chest, right where it belongs. But my mind...? Yes, I'd happily be mindless for this rock god.

'I want you.' He rips the condom out and slides it over his dick.

'Tell me something I *don't* know.' I laugh, and then his hands are beneath my arms, pulling me up even as I crawl higher over his body and straddle him, taking him and moaning as he thrusts into me.

I tilt backwards and stare at the ceiling as all the walls of my world implode.

I am lost.

'You know…' He runs a fingertip down my spine and I shiver, my body still in paroxysms of desire even now, ten minutes after we've both crested that glorious wave and felt the complete delight that follows absolute surrender to pleasure. 'You're very good for my ego.'

I smile against his chest, listening to his heart thumping solidly. 'Shouldn't that be the other way around? It's not every day I get seduced by a superstar.'

He runs his finger lower, curving it over the roundness of my ass.

'Is that what I am?'

'Uh-huh. Apparently.'

'I'm not sure I seduced you, though.'

I laugh. 'Seriously?'

'You were staring at me all night…'

'Was not!'

I push up onto my elbows and my hair falls over his chest, tumbling across his tanned skin. I drop my lips to the ridge between his pecs and kiss him slowly, tasting the tang of his sweat and the masculinity of his body.

My insides clench. He is warm; he is hot. I could stay here all day.

The very thought is a dangerous electrical current I must immediately subdue.

I don't do that. I *won't* do that. Sex is fine, but anything more is where things get tricky. I swallow, pretty sure confusion is in my smile as I pull away from him.

'Anyway, Mr Rock Star, I think this is where our time must end.' I sigh dramatically, doing my best impersonation of a Shakespearean actress, and stand up.

My clothes are spread like confetti over the carpet. I feel his eyes on me as I move through the room, watching me scoop the garments off the floor.

'Mind if I grab a quick shower?'

He doesn't answer straight away. His expression is vague, like he's not concentrating, or perhaps he hasn't even heard.

'Ethan?'

'Sorry—yeah. Right. Go ahead.' He nods towards the bathroom.

My body feels like it's been stripped raw. Every nerve-ending vibrates as I rub myself with a loofah, spreading suds across my skin and rinsing them away. In the past, whenever I had one-night stands, I used to feel the after-shower was almost ceremonial. A wiping away of what I'd done.

I don't feel that now.

Or, if I do, I feel it with regret.

I don't want to walk away from him. And that's a serious problem. I've only ever felt that one time in my life and it led to a verified disaster.

Jeremy almost broke me. *Almost?* I forgot how to function for *months* after it ended.

Following desire to the point of stupidity was almost the end of me.

I will never make that mistake again.

I flick the taps off and stand in the steamy cubicle for a moment, steadying myself for what comes next.

Goodbyes are never nice, are they?

I brace myself for the inevitable swapping of numbers as I dress. The promise to call. The certainty that neither of us will.

When I step out into the lounge area he's dressed in a pair of low-slung jeans and nothing else. His chest is a piece of art—and I should know, given what I do!—but it's his bare feet that I find strangely erotic. There's something so confident about the way he stands, legs wide, arms crossed—seriously gorgeous arms—his eyes fixed on the bathroom door as though he's been waiting for me to emerge. He's like a caged lion, and yet there's something inherently laid-back about him.

The second I step out heat erupts, like wildfire spreading across a desert. It burns all of me, all the way through. I smile brightly, pretending I'm fine. Pretending hard that I don't feel it.

'Sooo…' I move towards him, reaching for my purse. 'This has been fun.'

'Fun…yeah.' He nods, still with that same sense of distraction on his handsome face.

I lift up on tiptoes and kiss his stubbled cheek, then step back.

Goodbyes are *never* nice.

I fight an urge to say any of the things that people might say in this situation. *I'll call you…* Or *Let's do this again sometime…* Or, *If you're ever in town let me know…*

'Listen, Ally…'

He drags a hand through his hair and I catch a hint of his beautiful fragrance and almost groan.

How can I want him again?

No, it's not that I want him *again*. I *still* want him. I want to stay curled up in bed, my body wrapped around his. I want to eat ice cream off him until I can't eat any more.

Every thought like that is a brick against my side. I've been stupid before. I've lost my heart before. I've lost it in a way that taught me the most important lessons about myself and my life. My heart has been broken and I doubt it will ever fit back together again.

He's searching for words, searching my face too. Looking for a way to tell me what he needs to say.

'It's okay.' I rush the words out, my smile over-bright. 'Seriously, Ethan, it's okay. You don't need to say anything.' I reach for his hand and squeeze it. 'I'm not looking for anything more than last night. It was…perfect. Let's not do the whole swapping numbers thing, okay?'

Still his eyes roam my face, intuiting more from me than I want to share. My cheeks heat and I turn away, scooping up my bag and tucking it under my arm.

Props are a funny thing, aren't they? Just the simple act of putting my purse in place gives me an added layer of confidence, tethering me to myself and my feelings, reminding me of who I was before this night reached into my soul and swished everything up.

'Thank you,' he says, and I acknowledge the incongruity of that polite remark.

I spin and kiss him on his cheek once more. 'You're welcome.'

In the end I didn't say goodbye. I just walked away as though I was heading to the shops or out to get coffee. No biggie.

I walked away and didn't look back.

I couldn't. I fear one last peek might have killed my will-power.

She is everywhere I look in the room. I smell her on the pillow as I press my head into it, and when I close my eyes I see her.

Ally.

Ally naked, glorious, owning me, burning me.

Ally.

My gut twists as though I've cheated on my girl-friend. My *ex*-girlfriend, who is now the fiancée of someone else.

It doesn't change the way something strange is

shooting through me. Emotions that are hard to interpret. Anger. Jealousy. Resentment.

Relief.

And something I have to own as sinister.

Sienna would hate it that I fucked Ally.

And I think I kind of like that.

I check the details of my appointment once more,
wishing my assistant Lesley would proofread her
emails before sending them.

Two p.m. appuntment with Grayson Heynes. 44
West Eleventh, The Vilage. Complete renovashun.
Meet at address.

Her spelling is so bad that I've often wondered
how the hell she graduated from high school. But
what she lacks in her ability with the written word
she makes up for in every other way. Lesley is my
organisational guru, and she works harder than anyone I've ever known. No matter when I email her,
she writes back within minutes. She is calm and
strangely unflappable.

God knows I need her stability.

More now than usual.

I have to admit that since the weekend I've been
in a weird headspace. I went running twice—morning and night, both days. That's not completely out
of the ordinary, but it's been a long time since I've
pushed myself that hard.

Only I've found myself with an odd surplus of energy since that night with *him*.

I shy away from using his name.

It's as though my blood has been supercharged and I am a different person altogether. I look the same, but I'm not. It's really weird. And I don't welcome the feeling—not one little bit.

Jeremy taught me everything I need to know about relationships. I will never again let a man change who I am. I will never again let a man make me doubt myself.

I shiver. I've been thinking of Jeremy more lately than usual. That's Ethan's fault too... Maybe Eliza was wrong. I'm not ready for this. What's wrong with being celibate and alone anyway? I'm pretty sure I can get all my kicks from *Game of Thrones*.

Mmm... Jon Snow...

I feel nothing.

God, what kind of sexual spell has Ethan Ash cast over me that even invoking Jon Snow doesn't dull the memories of our night together?

I turn my head, scanning the street in one direction. Nothing. Just the buzz of normal West Village life. A woman with two small children and a Golden Retriever on one side of the street and a tourist couple on the other.

Neither of those looks like my new client.

I turn in the opposite direction just in time to see a man step out of a black limousine. He wears a suit but it barely contains his strength. He's short and broad, with close-cut blond hair, a golden tan, and he wears sunglasses despite the fact the day is bleak.

He moves towards me purposefully so I smile, glad I applied an extra layer of my favourite bright red lipstick.

'Miss Douglas?'

'Ally, please,' I say, extending my hand, trying to place his accent. Australian?

He nods in answer. 'This way.' He gestures to the door of the townhouse behind me and I have to fight my smile.

I *love* these brownstones. Like every woman my age, I grew up on *Friends* and *Sex and the City* repeats, and these buildings exemplify New York to me. It's why I love where *I* live, around the corner from here. Because I feel like I've walked onto the set of my favourite TV show and it's every bit as amazing as I thought it would be.

But a whole townhouse—no, *two*? He pushes the door open and we're right in a construction site. There are tins of paint, ladders, and yellow tape, presumably indicating 'no-go' areas.

'You're joining the two together?'

Excitement swarms through me. The cost of the real estate alone, and then these extensive renovations, indicate that Mr. Heynes has considerable finances at his disposal.

I take on many projects, for clients with varying degrees of wealth, but by far the most fun to work with are the couples or clients who are seriously loaded. Who let me go to town on assembling an art collection worthy of a world-class gallery. I suspect Mr. Heynes might just be one of them.

'This way, please.'

I fall into step beside him, breathing in the architectural beauty of the building as we go. I note with pleasure that someone has chosen to keep all the original features. Deco ceiling roses are in a state of restoration, so too the fancy balustrade that borders the stairs. We move deeper into the townhouse and the natural light that floods in from the back garden is exquisite. A grey day it might be, but this garden is both a sun-catcher and a green oasis in the middle of New York City.

A movement in the corner catches my eye and I'm drawn to it instinctively. Another man, sitting in a folding director's chair, stands up.

It takes my mind longer than my body to recognise who it is.

My body knows straight away, of course, as proved by the way my nipples strain against the fabric of my shirt, and the way all of me pulses with need. Memories of our night together flood my brain and desire is instantly, obviously heavy in the room.

Ethan Ash stares back at me, a sexy smile on his face, like he's waiting for me to speak. Or to jump him.

CHAPTER SIX

'ETHAN...?' THE WORD is an exhalation. A query, yes, but also a soft, muted groan.

He's wearing jeans again. The same ones he was wearing the day I left? Saturday? Four days ago? Is that all? But he's teamed them with a simple blue and white button-down shirt, the sleeves pushed up to reveal his tanned forearms, and he's got simple Nikes on his feet—nice shoes, but I miss his sexy bare feet instantly. His hair is in disarray, reminding me forcibly of how it looked after I'd run my fingers through it.

'Thank you, Grayson.'

The man I met outside nods. 'I'll be out front.'

I turn to face Mr. Heynes, but he's already disappearing back down the hallway we walked together.

'My bodyguard,' Ethan says, with a grin that is instantly disarming.

Usually I'd have something pithy to say in response to that, but I'm blindsided. Blindsided by the fact that I'm staring at the man I had the best sex of my life with—whom I thought I'd never see again.

I thank the fashion gods that I chose to wear my favourite black jersey dress today, teamed with sky-high Louboutins and a chunky gold necklace. It's an outfit that always leaves me feeling confident.

I haven't said anything in a really long time, and his smile has turned into a frown. A little line has dug its way between his thick brows.

I look away quickly, needing to gather my wits—urgently. 'What are you doing here?'

'It's my place,' he says simply, as though that explains everything.

I expel a sigh of frustration. 'That's not what I mean.'

'I know.' He moves towards me and the vibrations that are affecting me on a cellular level intensify sharply. My stomach swoops.

Great.

'How did you get my number?'

He doesn't look the slightest bit ashamed. 'I looked on the internet for art advisors with long red hair and hypnotic eyes. You were right there.'

I cross my arms over my chest, tapping my fingers at my elbows disapprovingly.

'You have an excellent reputation, Alicia.'

I arch a brow, ignoring the way his praise makes something pleasant spread through me. 'Why am I here?'

He stops right in front of me, so close that I can see all the flecks of black in his ocean-green eyes. 'I have a proposition for you. Two, actually.'

'A proposition?'

'Two.' He nods towards the garden, and for the first time I see a little table has been set up there. 'Have lunch with me.'

Swoop. Swoop. I'm on a rollercoaster of emotions. I tighten my seatbelt mentally, donning my best hyper-professional voice. 'There's really no need…'

His eyes pierce me all the way to my core. 'Lunch.'

He speaks so authoritatively his strength and dominant confidence slam into me, and I am completely powerless to resist his request.

I *shouldn't* stay. I know that. I should go. No, I should run. Because I'm looking at him, and what I really want to do is collapse against him, against his strong chest, press my ear to his heart and listen to its shudderingly wonderful rasp. What I really want to do is strip his clothes off his rock star body and touch him all over.

But I can't. I don't. That would be madness.

What was so natural and easy that night is now just out of my reach. We are not a couple. We are not even friends. We are strangers who fucked. Once.

No, not once, my memory hastens to correct me. We fucked the hell out of each other. But it was just *one* night. One glorious night.

I don't even realise I'm chewing on my lower lip until he reaches down and smudges his finger across it, pushing my hand away. Heat sears me and my eyes lock to his. I feel the earth shift beneath our feet. Does he as well?

'Lunch?'

I realise I haven't answered. Slowly, I nod my

head—so slowly that it's as though I've been drugged. And I kind of have been. *He* is a drug. And exposure is fast turning me into an addict.

'Okay.' I sound pissed off, and I am. I have dealt with my desire for him and I have boxed away what we were that night. Now I am looking at him again, and possibilities I dare not explore are twisting and turning inside me.

I have to be strong.

I can manage this.

I can control it.

It is a balmy day. The low cloud cover has layered humidity over the city and I'm pleased to see that he hasn't organised anything hot to eat. The table has some kind of yam salad on it, with what looks like feta cheese and herbs, and another salad. Kale?

And in the middle, so beautiful and attention-grabbing: a single peach.

'I remember what you like,' he says with a wink, and my blood boils. It's intentionally ambiguous, but I imagine he's not talking about the peach. I don't think I'll ever be able to look at a peach without re-membering the way Ethan Ash went down on me.

Against my will, my eyes run down his body, landing on his crotch. I'm not imagining the way he's straining against his pants, and I'm glad. Im-mediately glad.

If I'm going to be wading through sensual heat then he'd better damned well be doing the same.

'Good to know.'

His smile is droll as he pulls the chair out for me.

As I sit his hands brush my shoulders and my stomach lurches.

He pours us a couple of glasses of sparkling mineral water and I watch him. I watch everything about him. The way his thick hair flops forward over his brow a little, the way his fingers are firm and commanding as they wrap around the bottle. The way he is strong and confident and sexy even while undertaking such a mundane task. The way his eyelashes, long and thick, clump together.

It was like this with Jeremy, I remind myself. Desire made me dumb. It made me incapable of feeling anything else.

He looks up and smiles—a smile which drops slightly when he sees the look on my face. I imagine I look a little bit the way a wolf might stare at a lamb. I am hungry; he is my meal.

Or is it the other way around? Beneath the table he kicks out his legs and his foot brushes against my ankle. I can't tell if it's intentional or not, and it hardly matters. The effect is the same. The heat of the sun rampages through my system.

'So…' I say, desperate to regain some control of the situation. 'Why don't we cut to the chase?'

His eyes narrow, regarding me thoughtfully. As if he's trying to read my mood. 'I had fun the other night.'

I swallow, but it's no good. The beauty of that night burns me with its heat. 'Me too.' It's a raspy, cautiously given admission.

'I want to do it again.'

Alarm bells are screeching through me. *Again?* 'Why?'

His laugh is soft and he leans forward, his eyes hooked to mine. 'Seriously? You want a reminder?'

Heat flames my cheeks. 'It was a one-night-stand, Ethan. By definition, we're done.'

He nods thoughtfully. 'And that's what you want?'

'Get out of my house, you little whore!'

The way she spun around, her face puce, her hair black.

'Did you think you could bring her here and I wouldn't know? Jesus, Jeremy. Did you think I didn't smell her on the sheets? Our children will be home in ten minutes! Get her out of my house!'

I feel like I'm going to vomit. The horror of that lazy afternoon, of being woken up by my fiancé's wife, by the realisation that I'd bought his story hook, line and sink-me-sinker, tears through me. I'd looked at Jeremy and seen all my dreams, and he was actually a walking nightmare.

How easy it had been to believe his lies!

'I'm staying with my brother's family while my place is being renovated.'

It had been *his* family! *His* kids' drawings all over the fridge. *His* wife's photo on the landing. How foolish I was.

I told myself I'd never be so stupid again. That I would never be so caught up in a man that I forgot common sense and rational thought.

I don't want a relationship.

I don't even want sex.

It was only Ethan too-good-to-resist Ash that made me forget that.

For one night.

'Yeah.' I nod, but it's weak with uncertainty. 'Look, Ethan…' I sigh almost apologetically and a small part of my brain wonders how often Ethan Ash gets rejected. 'I'm not looking for a relationship. The other night was great, but it was just sex. Really, *really* good sex…'

He nods, a droll expression on his face. 'That's why this is perfect.'

'Why? What?'

'I don't want a relationship either.'

He sips his drink, keeping his eyes latched to mine the whole time. He replaces it on the table without breaking eye contact.

'I just want to fuck you.'

A lightning bolt of anticipation flashes down my spine. It is so tempting. And, hell, I want what he says *he* wants. I want to rip my clothes off and beg him to take me right there, on the manicured lawn and beneath the sultry grey sky.

But can we do that? Can we really just fuck without getting our emotions, all of ourselves, involved? I don't know if I have what it takes for that.

'It's too complicated.' I hear the prim rejection, and somewhere a part of me is glad that I have at least a degree of common sense.

'There's nothing complicated about what we feel,' he contradicts.

I shake my head. 'I can't get involved.'

'Why not?' His eyes narrow speculatively and he's tense suddenly. 'Are you with someone else?'

My heart turns over at the very idea. I shake my head, but the memories of my affair are too strong inside me. Being cast as 'the other woman' without my knowledge and without my consent. It is a wound I will probably always carry. It doesn't matter to Jeremy's wife that I had no fucking clue he was married. That he was a dad. I *slept* with her husband. I got *engaged* to the father of her children.

I broke up a family.

Guilt colours my cheeks and I feel the warning sting of tears out of nowhere. I push them back.

'Look...' He sighs again. 'I don't know if you heard about it—I mean, it was all over the news at the time. I broke up with my girlfriend a few months back.'

His eyes show torment when they meet mine: a torment that is matched by my swirling gut.

I tilt my head to the side, trying to remember. My Poldark knowledge is exceptional, so too my knowledge of Westeros family trees, but real-world drama...?

'It was completely messed up.' He shakes his head, as if dismissing tormenting thoughts of his own. 'The night I met you I'd just found out she got engaged.'

'And you were pissed?' I murmur.

It's not a question, but he answers anyway. 'That's an understatement. I wanted to tear the world apart.'

Something strange shifts inside me. 'How long were you together?'

He is quiet, and my experience with Jeremy reminds me that this is a sign of secrecy. That he's hiding something from me.

'Forget it,' I say sharply. 'It doesn't matter. I'm not getting in the middle of it.'

'She's engaged to someone else,' he says throatily, and I hear the emotional rawness in the words. 'There is no middle.'

'But you're still in love with her?'

The question catches him off-guard. It's as if he realises the inappropriateness of talking to *me*, the woman he's most recently-fucked, about the woman he loves.

'Hell, no. Right now I think hate would be a better word to describe what I feel for her.'

I discount that. I know that pain. I've felt it. 'You can love at the same time as you hate.'

'Speaking from experience?' he prompts.

'Yes.' It's both an admission and a warning. I'm shutting the conversation down.

He seems to understand that. 'Not with Sienna. Not after this.'

Sienna?

'Sienna Di Giorgio?'

Now I remember. It *was* in the papers at the time, and on news websites, and people were gossiping about it. It was a big deal to people who cared about that kind of thing—which was almost everyone.

'Have you spoken to her?'

'Nah.'

Jealousy curdles inside me. 'Maybe that's what you need? To get some closure?'

He laughs. 'Talking to Sienna isn't going to give me "closure".' And he stands up, his manner completely animalistic, wild, untamed, as he prowls to my side of the table. 'I want to fuck you.'

I startle at the bald-faced honesty of the statement.

'Rebound sex?' I prompt, some sense of self-preservation forcing me to face up to what he wants before this goes any further.

His eyes glint and I feel the determination of his heartbreak. I recognise it.

'Something like that.'

And I want to agree. To acquiesce. To give him all of myself.

But is there danger here? Am I being foolish?

'Just sex?'

'Just sex.' He nods, reaching for me and pulling me to stand.

We are body to body…so close. I hesitate and he strikes, moving even closer, speaking low and throaty.

'I…'

He brings his mouth to my ear.

'Want…'

He sucks my lobe between his teeth and then bites down on it. I pull in a breath.

'To…'

His fingers find the bottom of my dress and push it up my thighs until it's at my hips.

'Fuck…'

His hands curl around my ass and thrust me forward, holding me tight to his arousal. He grinds his hips and I groan as I remember how good he feels inside me.

'You.'

He hasn't even said the last word before my fingers are searching for the buckle of his belt and pushing it open. I want that too.

His ex. My ex. They cease to exist.

There is no one in my mind but Ethan Ash as I push at his jeans until they're open and then reach in and wrap my fingers around his cock.

'Shit…' he groans.

'This is crazy.'

'No,' he grunts. 'This is a proposition. You. Me. Sex. It's easy.'

He rubs his cheek against mine, his stubble coarse, and then he kisses me—hard, achingly, his tongue punishing mine, as though our four days apart were my fault. It is crazy and it is reckless and I know I might regret it, but I will regret stopping even more.

He pulls me as we kiss, in through the doors, but we've barely made it inside before we tumble to the hardwood floors, a tangle of clothes and hormones, of need and lust. He pushes me onto my back and I'm shaking as he slides a condom in place. I'm pushing at his jeans and he's sliding out of them, and all the while I'm chasing his mouth, not wanting our kiss to end.

He doesn't remove my underwear—who has time

for that? He pushes the flimsy lace aside and thrusts into me hard and fast, with all the desperation in the world, as though he knows how ready I am for him. And I am. So ready, so wet, so hungry. I cry out at his possession and arch my back, inviting him to touch me.

He doesn't need the invitation.

His hands are under my dress and he finds my breasts, rolling my nipples as he drives into me, and I am moving higher and higher above the earth with every touch, morphing out of this very plain of existence. I am all his...all this...all need.

It is a primal coming together. There is nothing slow or seductive about it. But I have never been more aroused. Even as I come I feel another orgasm building immediately afterwards, intense and powerful. I dig my nails into his hips, feeling his warm, smooth flesh and wanting to mark it with my possession of him.

I wrap my legs around his waist and he drops his hands to my ass, curving his hands beneath me and kneading my flesh until I groan into his mouth.

I am incapable of thought. I am incapable of anything but feeling. And I feel him everywhere. Each thrust drives him deeper into my body until I am existing purely for this. All for him.

And I'm just sensible enough to be afraid of that.

'You said two propositions?'

Our breathing is returning to normal. His body is a weight on me that I crave.

'Right.'

He grins slowly, sensually. My stomach flops.

'Do I take it that means you accept the first?'

I pull a face. 'I'm thinking about it.'

He nods thoughtfully. 'Might you need more convincing?'

My body trembles. 'I might.'

I don't. I want to sleep with him again and again—which should in and of itself warn me off.

Ethan shifts a little; my body responds instantly.

'I have a designer for the interior. But I want your artistic input. I want you to wave your magic wand over this place. Think you can do that? For me?'

The way he says that should warn me, but I am not afraid. We have been honest—we have immunised ourselves against emotional fallout. Flirting with him is fine because we both know what we want.

And what's at stake if we don't.

'You're asking me to work for you?'

He nods. 'Yes. What d'you say?'

I say *yes*, don't I?

'Why don't you show me the place while I make up my mind?'

'I guess this will be a kind of entertaining area.' He gestures around the large open space on the top floor of the townhouse. It's huge. Cavernous, even. I instantly see it as it could be. Neutral décor. Cream walls, polished floorboards and a single feature wall of a dark, earthy grey colour. Modern lighting, like round floor lamps and curved wall lamps, and perhaps a shag pile rug in the middle.

And contemporary art. Abstract without being corporate.

There's a Hirst I know Christie's has coming up for auction and mentally I picture it on the wall. I can't recall the exact dimensions off the top of my head, so I reach into my bag and pull out my iPad mini.

'What about something like this?' I load up the painting and hold the iPad closer to him. Not too close. Not so close that I can breathe him in or risk touching him.

What happened downstairs is still playing on the edges of my mind, and I don't know if I should run and hide or pretend it's business as usual. I've opted for the latter, but every movement he makes reminds me passionately of what we've done. What I want.

I struggle to make sense of it.

'I love it.'

He smiles as he meets my eyes. He's so straightforward and simple...it's hard to believe he feels anything like my inner-turmoil.

Why am I complicating things? We're two adults who want to have a no-strings-attached sex-fest. What danger is there in that?

I quickly spin away from him, not wanting him to see even a hint of my thought processes on my face.

The business with Jeremy scared me. For life, possibly. Well, Eliza says it fucked me up good, and I've always kind of agreed with her.

I fell in love with him hard and fast. And I thought it was mutual. I believed everything he told me. Six months into our relationship I should have seen the signs. The way he would often not answer my calls. The way he'd have weird explanations for what he'd been doing, and the way he'd change plans at a moment's notice. The way we once went to a restaurant and a couple came over to speak to him and the woman kept looking at me with obvious confusion.

And then, yes... The way his wife walked in on us *in flagrante*.

God, what an idiot I'd been.

So? Was I being an idiot now?

'How come you have such a huge place when you don't even live in the States?'

His shrug is non-committal, as though we're talking about a studio apartment rather than two brownstones joined at the seams.

'I like it here. And there are times when I do American tours and it would make sense to have a bit of a home away from home. You know? Plus, it's a good investment.'

I nod thoughtfully. 'Do you get sick of the travelling?'

'I try not to do too much of it.'

'But you tour...?'

'Yeah, I tour.' His smile is so sexy. 'But I get my agent to build in weeks of time when I get back home. To sleep in my own bed.'

To see Sienna?

I push the other woman aside. She's engaged.

They broke up months ago. This isn't like Jeremy and Fiona.

'I'd hate it,' I say thoughtfully.

Moving carefully, I step over a large gap in the floorboards into the other side of the room and towards the floor-to-ceiling windows that overlook the garden. Our lunch is still down there. My poor fork stabbed into a slice of yam, indignantly waiting to be wielded.

'Yeah?'

'Oh, yeah. I'm such a homebody.'

'I wouldn't have guessed that.'

'No?'

'No.'

He comes to stand beside me and I'm aware of all the things I don't want to be.

'I can't get involved with you,' I say, without meeting his eyes.

'Can't? Or don't want to?'

It's a distinction I hadn't even realised I'd made. I side-step it deliberately. 'I think you're trouble.' Now I force myself to look his way. 'And I'm not into that.'

He studies me without speaking. Then…

'But you used to be?'

I'm startled, blinking away my surprise. How can he tell?

I twist my lips to the side and shrug, just a little. 'Trouble used to be into *me*.' It's a subtle correction. 'I've learned to spot it.'

He doesn't say anything. We stare down at the garden—it really is very beautiful. My body is still tingling from the way we came together. We are dynamite and flame. On our own, innocuous enough. But together…?

We have no hope.

'And yet the idea of sleeping with you holds definite appeal.' I run my eyes across his handsome face, over his lips that drive me wild.

'*Sleeping* isn't part of the equation.' He winks and, heaven help me, my body—*all* of it—groans.

'Right.' I smile. 'And, you know, I wonder if we shouldn't just…have fun together.'

He expels a sigh of relief. 'Thank God for that.'

But I'm still not convinced this is a good idea. I'm still terrified of everything that could go wrong.

'How would this work? I mean, I really…*it* really has to be just sex. No strings.'

'Yeah…' He grins, scanning my face. 'We can do that.'

'But what if we can't? What if one of us wants more?'

He arches a brow. 'We won't.'

'How do you know?'

He shrugs. 'If it makes you feel any better, we'll put some ground rules in place.'

'Ground rules?' I nod slowly. It's a good idea, but I can't resist teasing him. 'You're disappointingly conservative for a rock star, aren't you, Mr Ash?'

'I'm afraid I might be,' he says, with a wink that makes my tummy roll and my body vibrate.

Nothing, I repeat, *nothing* about him is disappointing.

'Would you find the conversation more acceptable if I do this?'

And he kisses my neck, sending shoots of awareness through me. I nod, but coherent thought is becoming difficult. It's worse when he drops his hand beneath my skirt and finds my heated core, sliding his fingers deep inside me. I throb around him, groaning at the sweetness of the invasion.

'You were saying…' I whimper as pleasure builds, need intensifies.

'Ground rules…' The words are throaty.

'Right.'

I tilt my head back until it connects with the glass of the window. I am lost to pleasure once more. How can he do this to me? I read a *Cosmo* article years ago about the number of calories a woman burns when she comes. Was it sixty? A hundred? I'm going to need to up my carb intake while I'm fucking Ethan, that's for sure.

'What do you want from me?' he asks, his lips brushing the words into my mouth.

I shiver; it's so sensual.

'Fun,' I grunt back as pleasure intensifies and thickens around me. 'Just fun.'

'No flowers? No sleepovers? No expectations beyond satisfaction?' he teases. 'Nothing serious?'

'God, no. *Fun.*' I dig my fingers into his hips. 'Fuck, Ethan, I'm…'

He withdraws and my eyes fly open, finding his. Outrage trembles inside me, but only for a moment— because then he's crouching on his haunches and his mouth is against me, his tongue demanding that my pleasure continues.

'Oh, God…' My fingers dig into his shoulders now and all my weight is against the window.

Please, don't let it break.

But would I even care? What a blissful way to go.

'What else?' he asks my clit, so that I can't help but laugh.

It's quickly subdued by a keening cry of need. He's *so* good at this. *So* good at everything.

'It's just temporary…' I can hardly speak now. I don't want to talk. I don't want to think. Feelings are carrying me away. 'How long are you…' I pause, trying to catch my breath '…in the States for?'

'Two weeks.'

'Okay.' I nod, but I am losing my mind with pleasure. 'That's our end-date.'

And that's it. That's all she wrote.

I cannot form more words or thoughts or objections. I vibrate against the window and against him and he holds me tight, kisses me until the wave has calmed. He knows what I need; he expresses that knowledge with every movement of his body and his mouth.

I am afraid and yet I am fearless. I am a contradiction in his arms, against his wall, in his house.

And then he stands.

'You've got yourself a deal.'

CHAPTER SEVEN

'WHO THE FUCK is she?'

I'm groggy, and it takes me a second even to recognise it's Sienna's voice coming from my phone.

'Who is who?' I rub a hand over my eyes and
then flop back on the bed. 'Sienna, it's five o'clock
in the morning.'

'Who is the woman you're with?'

I think of Ally instantly and flip over, reaching for
her on autopilot. She's not there. Of course she isn't.

No sleepovers.

'What woman?'

'Oh, I'm sure there's a billion. I'm talking about the
one on all the gossip sites today. With the red hair.'

The photo. Taken the night we hooked up. It's
online?

Curiosity has me putting my phone on speaker, so
that I can load up a browser without cutting Sienna off.

'Are you *kidding* me? You're engaged. Why the
hell do you care who I'm fucking?'

Sienna's sharp intake of breath is audible. 'So you
are fucking her?'

Bingo. My gut clenches. You can't see Ally's face but it's obviously her. There's something so elegant about her, even in the paparazzi shot. Her long hair is tossed over one shoulder and her face is averted. My hand is clutched possessively around her.

My eyes narrow. 'Yeah. You'd better believe I am.'

'Jeez, Ash. *Classy.*'

'*You* can talk! You didn't think you owed me a heads-up before you Tweeted the whole goddamned world with your engagement news?'

She's quiet. I wonder if she's feeling guilty and then discount it. Sienna is selfish. Singularly so.

'I shouldn't have done that.'

It's something. But it's not enough. This typifies our relationship. Her spectacularly bad behaviour followed by an almost-apology. Always insufficient, and yet I always let her get away with that.

Not any more.

'Damn straight. What were you *thinking*?'

'We'd had a few bottles of Bolly,' she murmurs. 'I don't think I really *was* thinking. Anyway, you're no better.'

'Because I'm sleeping with someone else? In the privacy of my hotel?'

'Oh, don't expect me to believe it's just *one* girl. I've seen the way they chase after you. I imagine you're engaged in nightly orgies by now.'

I laugh. 'If that's what you want to imagine me doing, go right ahead.'

An orgy would have nothing on what Ally offers.

I lie back against the pillows and close my eyes.

I remember the way she went down on me, her huge eyes looking up at me. My dick clenches.

'You're such a bastard…' Sienna sniffs.

'Yeah, well, just as well you don't have to put up with me any more.'

I disconnect the call and toss my phone aside. It's far more fun to imagine Ally's lips around my cock than it is to argue with Sienna.

But the conversation has unsettled me. Our break-up was bad. No—it was so much worse than that.

I have vague recollections of Sienna pitching a crystal vase at me as she shouted, and I remember saying awful things to her. Things I regret.

We were both so angry.

We were both aware that we'd been holding on to something that had at one time been good, but that had soured slowly. As if poison had been dripping into our relationship for years and we didn't want to acknowledge it.

Our final fight was proof of that.

There had been no love left.

I regret the way we ended it. Most of the time we were together it was okay, even good, and we knew each other in a unique way, both having gone from normality to immense fame almost overnight.

Which means we should have known better than to take our fight into the street. Well, that was Sienna, actually, storming out in the middle of the afternoon, mascara running down her cheeks, bare feet, shouting at me as though the world needed to know our issues.

Yeah, the break-up had been shit.

I get up and pull on some boxers, moving to my guitar on autopilot and staring out at Manhattan.

Things with Sienna are messed up, but that's okay. Because what I've got going with Ally is just perfect for where I'm at. Fucking someone normal and undemanding. Someone who seems even less interested in the whole romantic dating bullshit than I am.

No flowers.

No dating.

Just sex.

With a reassuring end-date that takes all the *Where are we going?* crap out of the equation.

Suddenly I'm as impatient as all hell to see her.

So, I've been thinking...

I send the text to Ally with a smile on my face, not expecting to hear back. It's so early she's probably still fast asleep.

The idea fills my imagination very pleasantly.

I place my phone down on the coffee table, beside my bare feet, and reach for my guitar. It's never far from me when I'm working on new songs, and I've been doing that for a month in earnest.

I begin to strum, and all I can think of is her smile. *Ally.*

Her name whooshes out of me. I lean forward and scrawl lyrics in my own particular brand of can't-be-fucked shorthand that will only ever be decipherable to me, note the chords, then lean back and stare out of the window, singing the lines over and again.

My phone buzzes.

Just in general? Or about something specific. Because I think you should be worried if you're ever *not* thinking.

She puts a little kiss emoji at the end and it reminds me so much of her that my grin threatens to split my face.

Oh, my thoughts are very, very specific.

Three little dots appear, to show that she's typing back, but then they disappear again. I grin, put the phone down and return to my guitar, continue playing. But after ten minutes, when she hasn't replied, I'm impatient to hear from her.

I pick the phone up and am about to start typing when a message swishes onto the screen.

Specifically...?

I laugh.

Ten minutes for one word? Seriously?

Her dots move frantically.

Are you literally standing by your phone waiting for me to reply?

Everything inside me tightens. This is *fun*. The kind of fun I haven't had in...years?

I think of Sienna with guilt. When did I stop finding her fun? Or is that normal after you've known someone a really long time?

Yep. Aren't you?

I stare out of the window, waiting for her to reply. It doesn't take long.

My prayers are answered. She's sent a photo of herself, a smiling photo taken as she...*runs*? Is she *running*? I pinch the picture. It looks to be a park somewhere. She has earphones in and a cap pulled low.

Even like this, with no make-up, her face pink from exertion, she is so beautiful. I ache for her.

Nice. How about you run my way next?

I briefly question the wisdom of such an obvious bootie call but her response is immediate.

I'll be there in ten.

Thank fuck.

Ethan Ash doesn't walk. He saunters. He saunters like the rock 'n' roll sex god he truly is.

I watch him from my vantage point on the other side of the foyer of the Gramercy Park Hotel, and every sauntering sexy step he takes makes my temperature heat and my blood boil, so that by the time he stops in front of me I am a hot puddle of lava on the expensive leather seat.

'Hey, you.'

Jesus. It should be illegal to be that sexy.'

He bursts out laughing and I fear I'm crab-pink all over, colour heating my cheeks all the way to my hairline as I realise I've said the words out loud. I briefly question the sense in coming to him like this—straight from a run. Should I have gone home and showered first? Done my hair and make-up?

He sobers, taking pity on me. And he leans down. 'Right back atcha.'

The kiss he presses against my cheek is chaste. My body doesn't get the memo, though, and every single cell inside me seems to vibrate and tremble and squeal in anticipation. With his lips beside my ear he whispers, the words husky, 'You in Lycra is something I'm never gonna forget.'

Desire pitches through me, rolling my stomach. I stand up on legs that are somewhat wobbly and almost collide with him. Almost? I *want* to collide with him. It's only his quick movement that saves us from bumping together, and he puts a hand in the small of my back. It is a touch of possession and it sparks my blood.

My eyes lift to his; in his face is the same heat as fills my body.

'Shall we?'

I nod, not sure I can speak in that moment.

His grin is my further undoing. It spreads across his face and all the while his eyes hold mine and I am sinking, incapable of staying afloat.

Another couple is waiting for the lift and they obviously recognise Ethan don't-forget-I'm-a-celebrity Ash. I step away, my smile tight, my body language instantly businesslike.

His teasing grin is all the indication I need that he has noticed.

I stare straight ahead, ignoring the obvious looks of appraisal from the other woman. When the elevator doors open they move in ahead of us. I step to the back of the lift and stay there, while Ethan leans nonchalantly against the panel of buttons, a hint of amusement obvious in every single one of his features.

'What?' I say, as soon as they step out and we are alone.

'You're embarrassed to be seen with me?'

'No.' I force a smile. 'There was a photo of us in the papers this morning.'

'The papers?' He frowns. 'I knew it was online.'

'It's *online*?'

My heart thumps. It's okay. *It's okay.* The woman in the picture doesn't look like me. Only it's not okay, because I can't bear putting my mom and dad through yet another scandal.

They're definitely not over the whole Jeremy thing. I think they took it harder than I did. Not just that I'd been 'the other woman' but that I'd been a homewrecker too. He had *kids*, for Chrissakes.

If they find out I'm in a purely sexual fling with a superstar like Ethan Ash they'll actually disown me.

'Mmm.'

He closes the space between us and I stay where I am, my back to the wall. My breath feels heavy somehow, weighted in such a way that it's dragged down instead of pushed out. His body presses against mine, but he doesn't touch me with his hands. Those he uses to brace himself against the wall of the lift, one on either side of me. He is the cage but my desire is untameable. It fills the cube we are in, surrounding us completely like a dense fog.

The doors open and he steps back from me, reaching for my hand and pulling me after him, out into the carpeted hallway. It's deserted, thank God, because I don't want to pull away from him again. We move quickly, the same silent force motivating our movements, making us step in haste.

He slips the key into the door and then pushes it wide. 'After you, Miss Douglas.'

'Thank you, Mr Ash.'

I step into the room and the table we first made love on—no, *fucked* on—is right in front of me. I walk towards it on autopilot, propping my hips against its edge, trailing my fingertips over the glass. Memories spike my blood. He's watching me, and that knowledge makes me smile.

He prowls towards me and lifts my baseball cap off my head. I briefly wonder how badly my hair is plastered to my head—particularly when his eyes continue their mapping of my features.

He lifts both hands and cups my cheeks, then runs his hands back to the elastic band holding my thick mane in a ponytail. He pulls at it determinedly, his eyes focused on the job so that I am able to focus on him. On the thumb-print-sized divot in his chin. The little score between his brows. The colours in his eyes that have mesmerised me from the first moment I saw him.

My breath escapes as a sigh and his lips twist in acknowledgement of the noise.

His fingers find the hem at the bottom of my shirt and push it up, just enough for his fingertips to glance my flesh. His touch is strangely reverent, as though he is worshipping at the altar of *me*. It has to be said that if I were ever granted deity status I would totally spend my time doing this.

His eyes roam my face, but he says nothing. He just stares at me for a long, cold second, and then his fingers find me again, and this time they lift my shirt all the way up, over my face, discarding it on the table top.

I'm wearing a neon green sports bra and it's glued to my skin. He slides his fingers under the elastic at the back and loosens it, but before he attempts to remove it he kisses me. It is a kiss of such depth and need that my gut twists. It is a kiss of ownership, of punishment, of anger and of conquest. Oh, and passion, too. So much passion.

I wrap my legs around his waist, holding him tight. His cock is hard. I feel him through my clothes and I moan into his mouth…a moan that must convey everything I want, because he picks me up, holding me to him, carrying me through the suite towards the bedroom.

He eases me to the ground and removes my bra at the same time, sliding it over my head. I laugh as it catches my hair.

He doesn't.

His mood is serious.

Focused.

A stone drops through me.

Is this about wanting me? Or wanting *her*? The night we met, he was furious with her. And he wanted me. For *me*? For myself? Or was it payback? Did he want to hurt her by fucking me?

So what? I remind myself. This is exactly what I want. Sex. Hot sex. No-strings sex.

It is a swift coming together. We fuck like two people who have been kept apart for months. There is a furious hunger in our movements that burns brightly and explodes swiftly.

He holds me tight afterwards, holds me against his chest, kisses the top of my head and strokes my hair.

'So, break it down for me. What's all the fuss about?'

He slides another piece of peach between my lips. I take it, savouring the juicy sweetness without looking at him.

'We've watched two episodes. How can you not *get* it?'

'Maybe I've been a bit distracted.'

He reaches over and catches a dribble of peach juice that's running down my chin. My cheeks flush.

I sigh with mock exasperation. 'It's just so *angsty*. I mean, he's been away at war, and everyone thought he was dead. His poor fiancé has had to grieve his loss and move on with her life—which she's done, by deciding to marry, let's face it, an obviously very poor second choice. Then he comes *back to town*!'

He's staring at me as though I've begun to talk in a foreign language.

'It's essentially a fight between good and evil! It's a drama, and, yes, there's romance, but it's *so…* Oh, forget it.'

He shrugs. 'It's just kind of boring.'

'How can you not *get* it?' I'm outraged. It is *so* not boring.

He slices another piece of peach, and though I'm facing forward I can see him in the periphery of my vision, his fingers lean and insistent, the paring knife wielded expertly.

I turn to him as he lifts the fruit, my lips parted. He slides it in but I wrap my lips around his finger, holding it in my mouth a moment while my eyes meet his.

'Plus,' I say quietly, pulling away, 'Aidan Turner is seriously hot.'

His brows shoot upwards. '*This* guy?'

'Uh, *yeah*.'

I turn back to the screen, smiling to myself as I hear the cogs turning.

'I mean, sure…if brooding and honourable is your thing.'

'I think it's kind of *every* woman's thing,' I say without looking at him.

'Careful, Alicia.'

My expression is one of innocence. 'What's wrong?'

He straddles me quickly, surprising me, and holds the last piece of peach to my mouth. I bite around it, but he pulls his fingers away this time, disposing of the stone and then reaching for the remote. He silences *Poldark* as he crushes his lips to mine. I taste peach and imagine he does too.

'Nothing's wrong.' He drags my lower lip between his teeth. 'I just don't want to share you with Poldark.'

I grin against his mouth even as a warning bell bleats in my brain. He's just joking. Being silly. Distracting me from a show he doesn't like. And I'm more than willing to be distracted.

'Stay the night.'

I'm on the brink of sleep.

Time has ceased to have meaning. We have been in his bed for hours. Talking. Dozing. Kissing. My body is an odd mix of weightlessness and heaviness. I am satiated and needy.

'What day is it?'

I'm only half joking. The week has passed so quickly that I can barely remember where I'm at.

'Saturday. Tomorrow's Sunday.'

He traces a finger down my nose, following the curve, lifting it over the small jump at its tip and then pressing it to my lips. I kiss it and he smiles beside me, then runs his finger onwards, over my chin to the cleft between my breasts.

Goosebumps scatter across my flesh.

'Ally?'

'Mmm?' I rouse myself to pay better attention.

'Stay tonight.'

'No sleepovers, remember?'

'Mmm… But you feel so *good*.'

He roves his hand over my naked breast, finding my nipple and circling it until I suck in a shuddering breath.

There is danger in spending the night. I know I must go. And I will. Soon.

I am no longer capable of thought, speech or staving off exhaustion. My eyes sweep shut.

I fall asleep with his hand on my breast and memories of him in my mind.

CHAPTER EIGHT

Where are you?

I PUSH MY phone back into my bag without answering, determinedly turning my attention to the flowers before me.

Stalls line the footpath, but I have my favourite, and I am nothing if not faithful. I select two bunches of tulips—yellow and pink—and hand over some cash from my back pocket. I cradle them against my chest as I weave through the markets, pausing to buy a pretzel and a coffee which I must juggle in one hand.

It's worth it. The pretzel is warm and soft, the dough salty on the outside and almost sweet within. The pretzel is a perfect metaphor for New York, this city that I found so impenetrable at first and which I now adore.

I have been wandering the streets for over an hour, wondering that same thing. I feel my phone buzz, but have no choice but to ignore it. My hands are now full.

It will wait.
Just sex.
No flowers.
No sleepovers.
No romance, no commitment.
No hassles.
No potential for heartbreak.

I smile resolutely and weave my way through people and stalls, puppies and children, and turn into my own street. Familiarity makes my heart skip a beat or two. I tell myself I am happy to be here, that I want to be in my own home rather than in his hotel room.

Yesterday was fun, but staying there again today would be habit-forming, and I'm not prepared to do that. I tell myself it was *smart* to sneak out while he was asleep, without so much as kissing his cheek for fear that it would wake him, and he would kiss me back, and then all my good intentions would be scarpered.

I reach the front door at the same time as Kelvin Monteith from the upstairs apartment is leaving; he holds it open and offers to carry the flowers up for me. I shake my head and climb the stairs, jiggling my key into the slot and pushing the door inwards.

Eliza's still asleep, but Cassie is in the kitchen, fixing breakfast. I can smell the bacon the second I step inside.

'Morning!' I call cheerfully, waving the tulips in her face. 'Aren't these beautiful?'

She arches a brow and taps her foot pointedly. 'What?'

'Well?'

'Well, what?'

'Have you been with *him* again?'

I shake my head. And then I shrug. 'Yeah.'

'That's three times this week?'

Heat suffuses my cheeks. 'Who's counting?'

She watches me for a long moment and then expels a sigh. 'Ally…'

'I know.'

I lay the flowers down on the bench and stretch on my tiptoes to rescue a glass jar from above the fridge. I half-fill it with water, and am about to stuff the flowers in when Cassie retrieves the jar and tips the water out. As she begins to wipe the inside of it I note the visible watermark with a wry smile. Trust Cassie to see such a small detail.

Cassie and Eliza were with me at my lowest ebb. Their concern is natural. But I am not going to be hurt again.

'This is different.'

'Yeah, well…*duh*. There can't be *two* men in the world as misogynistic and narcissistic as Jeremy.'

We all read a lot of psychology self-help books after the Jeremy incident. He stood as a cautionary tale for all of us. I have no doubt he will move into urban myth in time. *Bastard*.

And yet, despite all the metaphorical wounds he inflicted, I still rail against an instinct to defend him. Such was his power over me, I suppose, that even now I am somewhat in his thrall. How can I hate him but not want others to do so?

'Ethan's nice,' I say instead, definitely not adding that I'm pretty sure he's using me to get over Sienna Di Giorgio.

'Uh-huh.' Cassie's caution is understandable. 'Just…be careful.'

I nod, and my eyes meet hers reassuringly. I can't begrudge her concern. Cassie and Eliza had to scrape me up off the floor after Jeremy—they had to wipe my broken heart from the walls of our lives.

'I really, really am fine, Cass.'

After all, what could be more cautious than contractually agreeing to the terms of our arrangement prior to undertaking an affair?

'Okay.'

She reaches forward and bites my pretzel. Such is our friendship that I don't complain, even though I live for these damned things. I hand it to her and sip my coffee, and when I think she's distracted by turning the bacon I fish my phone from my pocket and swipe it open.

Be still my beating heart.

It's a photo of him. He's wearing a simple white singlet and it looks like that favourite pair of jeans. He's pulling a confused face and the rumpled bed is behind him. In his hand he's holding a peach. My gut clenches.

Come back?

I stare at the photo for several more seconds. The slick of desire is unmistakable. I enjoy its possession of my body because I feel it with the certainty that I will be with him again. *Soon.*

When I have proved to myself that I can stay away.

Being cat-called on the streets of New York is frustratingly common. So when I step out of work Tuesday evening and hear a wolf-whistle I straighten my spine and keep going.

'Hey, sexy!'

The voice is familiar. I stop walking and turn slowly, my eyes catching the limousine and Grayson immediately. The window is down just far enough for me to make out Ethan's hair and eyes and it's all I need. My tummy flops.

I pull on my handbag strap and walk towards the car. 'Hey.'

'Your chariot awaits, m'lady.'

I arch a brow. Emotions war inside me. Pleasure at seeing him, sure. But also worry. Worry that this isn't part of our deal.

'My chariot can go on its way,' I say. 'I like to walk.'

'Ah.' He nods slowly. 'But I have a surprise.'

I roll my eyes. 'I don't like surprises.'

'I think you'll like this one.'

He pushes the door open an inch. I'm tempted to walk away, but I've stayed away from him for two nights, so I've sort of proved myself capable of handling this…haven't I?

'What's the surprise?'

I slide into the limousine and instantly I'm over-powered by his proximity. The smell of him, the pos-sibility that I'll soon be touching him.

I buckle up in the seat beside him. 'Ethan?'

'You'll see.' He grins cryptically, then leans closer. 'You look good enough to eat.'

Grayson is behind the wheel. He starts the engine and then pulls out into the traffic. I watch the build-ings pass in a blur, curiosity as to where we're going lasting the entire drive.

Well, almost the entire drive. I recognise the ap-proach to the MoMA a few blocks out. I have spent so much of my time here since arriving in NYC that it is almost like a second home.

I love it.

But I do not love the idea of being here *now*.

Not when Ethan Ash hasn't kissed me in days. Not when Ethan Ash hasn't fucked me in days. Not when we could be back in his hotel, doing all the things I've been fantasising about all afternoon.

'Well?'

I step out of the car, staring up at the building with grudging admiration. From this vantage point it is modern and it is beautiful, but my favourite place to admire it from is two blocks away, from where you can see the higgledy-piggledy arrangement of the various levels, all precariously balanced on top of one another. Like a three-year-old might build a high-rise.

I could write a thesis on what that incautious, ir-reverent juxtaposition means. The balancing of lines and order with chaos and random-seeming placement. The way it makes sense even when it shouldn't.

'You look at this place like I'm looking at you,' he observes with sensual heat.

'Like I'm a mix of order and disarray?'

'Something like that.' His wink is a flirtatious whip across my spine. 'Shall we...?'

Desire to be alone with him is fighting a battle—and losing—with my love for this place. I nod and move towards the entrance, the pull of the gallery strengthening with every step.

Grayson has procured us some kind of special entry. We don't queue, and a museum staffer greets us. She is a stunning young woman, with caramel skin and chestnut hair, enormous brown eyes and an impressive cleavage barely contained by her museum uniform. Her eyes cleave to Ethan in a way that makes me think she wishes it were her body, not just her gaze.

An unpleasant tang of adrenalin flavours my mouth. My sense of anticipation is somewhat dimmed by the prospect of being accompanied by *anyone* other than Ethan but that's not why I stiffen.

Ethan Ash is seriously hot.

Hot in that way that is unusual and distracting. Hypnotic. He is also hugely famous. And he's here with me. But in the space of a little over a week he won't be. In a little over a week he'll be with someone else. Making love to someone else. Charming the pants off them with his husky voice and smile. Someone like this obviously very willing museum staffer.

My jealousy is misplaced, and yet it's real.

When he dismisses the woman with, 'Miss Douglas is an art expert. I'll be fine in her capable hands,' I am childishly relieved.

'Oh, sure, no problem. But you just shout out if you need anything at all, okay?'

'So, is this how it is for you?' I ask as we walk away. 'All special entry and people tripping over themselves to serve you?'

He grins at me and reaches for my hand, squeezing it in a way that speaks once more of intimacy and closeness. I squeeze back.

He grins. 'Nah.'

'Nah?'

'Where to?'

We pause outside the sculpture garden and I nod towards the stairs. 'Contemporary, of course.'

'Why *of course*?' he asks, taking my lead and walking with me.

'I like to start at the end and work my way backwards.'

I smile up at him and I'm shy suddenly. It's inexplicable; I don't like it. I look away, focusing on the wall ahead. This isn't a first date. It's an aberration. A distraction.

'It's easier to make sense of contemporary art in some ways. It speaks to people because it fits within the sphere of our current tastes and wants.'

'Not me,' he says with a shake of his head. 'Give me the Impressionists any day.'

My lips twist in acknowledgement but I try to hide my cynicism.

He sees it regardless. 'What? You don't approve?'

I select my words with care. 'The Impressionist movement is probably the most adored of all.'

'So I can't like it because everyone else does?'

'You can like whatever you like,' I demur. 'I'm just saying that its accessibility gives it a head start. Sunflowers. Lily pads. They're borrowed from so heavily in popular culture. You can see Monet splashed through airport advertising. People don't necessarily *like* the Impressionists so much as recognise them.'

He clutches a hand to his chest in mock pain and stops walking.

'What?'

I look around. Luckily no one is watching us.

'You *wound* me,' he says with exaggerated complaint.

'I'm sorry.' I grin, showing I feel no such thing. 'I'm always unstintingly honest.'

'You're wrong.' He sobers almost instantly and catches my hand. 'Let me show you.'

I resist the urge to point out *I'm* supposed to be giving *him* the tour, and willingly go with him, up several more flights of stairs, until a sign points us towards the Impressionists wing.

Despite everything I have just said I pause as we step into the hall, instantly overpowered by the beauty and profound uniqueness of each and every piece before us.

Ethan looks at me, and then continues to move slowly, skimming his eyes over each piece of art until finally he stops in front of a lesser-known Matisse.

Woman Reading, the caption proclaims.

'This was the first painting I ever loved.'

I look from him to the painting in surprise. 'Why?'

'There's something about it that speaks to me. Perhaps it's the way her back is turned. The whole painting is almost disdainful. The composition confusing. And yet the way I'm kind of...*excluded* makes me *want* to intrude. To tap her on the shoulder; make her look at me.'

He is describing a sense that is so perfectly what I think Matisse was aiming for that I want to kiss him.

Art-speak is not something everyone is comfortable with, and the fact that Ethan über-sexy Ash can do it so well is incredibly desirable.

'That's good,' I say, wondering at the catch of feeling in my voice. 'Art *should* create that kind of emotion in you. An emotional response is all that matters—no matter what inspires it.'

'So I'm allowed to like the Impressionists again?' he teases, all cerebral philosophising over and done with.

'I suppose so.'

And so, amongst the Van Goghs, Mondrians, Monets and Seurats, we begin our tour of the MoMa...

'Okay,' he says after we've finished two full floors. 'I showed you mine. What's yours?'

'My what?' I'm genuinely confused.

'Your favourite piece in here?'

Holy crap, she's hotter than Hades when she's talking about art.

I thought I might have lost her with my waffling on about *Woman Reading*, but if anything it spurred her on. As though she thought she was speaking to a kindred spirit—someone who understands her love of art.

And, Jesus, listening to her, I think I might.

Ally Douglas could explain *anything* to me and I'd be somewhat spellbound. I stare at her as she discusses the way light and shade have been used to create an apparent three-dimensionality to the simple painting, but all I can think about is the light and shade in her face, and the multi-dimensionality in her eyes as the late-afternoon sun cuts through the glass and settles freely on her face.

I think about the light and shade in her voice, too—the way it pitches and rolls with emotion as she moves along the exhibit, teaching me effortlessly. Not because she wants me to learn, or because she thinks I should know this stuff, but because she can't help herself.

Art is her passion.

And she feels passionately.

I listen to her patiently even as I am burning up. We reach the end of the display and there is only a red fire alarm on the wall. I want to tell her how beautiful she is. I want to tell her she's the most beautiful woman I've ever seen.

It's not just that. I want to do more of *this*. I like being out with her. Holding her hand. I like the idea of taking her to dinner. I want her to come to my concert and to be waiting backstage for me.

The arbitrary boundaries we've insisted on are annoying me now, and I know why.

I don't like it that Ally is making an art form out of pushing me away, walking away from me when it suits her. I have an insatiable need to unsettle the ease with which she does that. To unsettle her a little bit. Why? To make her forget about our rules? Just for a while?

Stuff it.

I lean closer and murmur, 'You're beautiful.'

Her head whips up to mine so fast I briefly worry she might have dislocated something. She stares at me but says nothing. I could get lost in those damned eyes of hers.

Then, as if reading my mind, she blinks and looks away, withdrawing herself from me.

'That's it.' Her voice is gravelled.

I can't take my eyes off her face immediately, but she lifts a finger and points and I am drawn to the gesture. I follow the direction until my eyes land on a portrait across the room.

It is of a woman with pale skin and rust-coloured hair. It's painted in profile and there's an enigmatic twist to her lips that prompts curiosity. I reach for

Ally's hand, still outstretched, and move us towards the picture.

'Your favourite?'

'Yeah.' The admission is softly spoken.

I look down at her; she's blushing. Is she annoyed with me?

Objectively, Ally is stunning. *Always*. But when her face flushes with colour she glows with all the warmth in the world and she is unlike anything I've ever seen. Even in the midst of this art she is…*intriguing*. A mix of intelligence, maturity and vulnerability.

An ache spreads through me, pervasive and hungry. There are too many people around for me to do what I want—to wrap her in my arms and kiss her as though my literal survival depends upon it.

'Why?'

She bites down on her lip and her eyes flick first to me and then away. 'Oh, I just really like it.'

She pushes the conversation away with tangible determination.

'They're going to be closing soon. We should go.'

CHAPTER NINE

I FEEL AS THOUGH the lift isn't moving.

Ethan is beside me, and we are being pulled upwards by cables and knots, but I *need* him. I need
him to fuck me. Not to tell me I'm beautiful. Not to
wander through the MoMA with me, looking at pictures and listening to me explain them.

That's breaking the rules!

What the hell were we thinking?

We have to fuck, and now, to remind us both of
all the things we want from this—and all the things
we *don't*.

When the doors finally open I can't help but groan
my relief. He grins at me and wraps an arm around
my waist, pulling me into his side, leading me down
the corridor towards his room. The second we are
inside I launch myself at him, holding him tighter,
seeking his mouth.

He seeks mine back. Our need is mutual. Urgent.
Inflammatory.

'Fuuuuck.' He rips himself away and stares at me
like he's trying to make sense of this, of me, of our

need. 'Fuck.' He shakes his head. 'What the hell are you doing to me?'

I don't want to talk. Even about sex and our insatiable need for it. I push myself against him, kissing him, pushing at his shirt, and he answers in kind, lifting my dress over my ass, higher, breaking the kiss just enough to undress me completely.

His fingers are demanding as they slide into the waistband of my underpants, pushing down, curving around my ass, and then he lifts me easily, as though I weigh nothing. He lifts me, and I wrap my legs around his waist, and his kiss is warming me up from inside. He lies me on the sofa but stays on top of me, and his kiss, the weight of his body, the roll of his hips—it is everything.

I arch my back, seeking him, needing him, but there are too many clothes in the way.

'Need...' I whimper, snapping his belt open and pulling it out of his jeans.

He reaches down and undoes his button and zip and kicks his legs out of the pants, barely breaking our kiss. His lips move over mine. His tongue is daring me, daring mine, taunting me, making me forget all my reasons for keeping this light. Making me want more, want to beg him to stay in my life in some capacity even when I know that temporary is all we are—all that makes sense.

Also all I should want.

I run my fingers up his back and he grunts; I think he swears but the ringing bell of desire is all I can hear. And our own urgent breaths, tangling together, the sound of the impatient passion that defines us.

He hums in my ear, and I make a sound a bit like a moan. He is so sexy—his voice so beautiful, so raw, so famous. It hits me then, for the first time, that I'm sleeping with a celebrity. Someone so famous that everyone in the world must know who he is.

And I pull back a little—just enough to see his face, to look into his eyes.

Fuck. What am I doing?

My heart trips over a little, thumping hard against my ribs, and my stomach swirls with emotions I don't even want to think about analysing. Recognition pulses through me. Why has it taken me so long to realise that he's not just Ethan? To remember that he's Ethan Ash, superstar?

'What is it?'

His gravelly voice travels through me, finding every space inside me and warming it up. Superheating me from the inside out.

I shake my head, but a frown lingers on my lips. I kiss him to chase it away, losing myself once more in the sensual charge that besieges us both.

'Are you okay?'

I nod, jerkily. 'Fuck me.'

His laugh is without humour. 'Alicia…?'

Oh, great. *Now* he goes and brings my real name into it.

'I'm fine,' I say, digging my fingers into his hips, dragging him down against me, lifting myself up in a wordless invitation.

But he breaks away from me and for a second I think he's not going to give me what I need. I am empty and bereft. But he returns a short moment later, a condom in his hand and a smile on his lips.

'You, Alicia Douglas, are a mystery.'

My heart twists. 'A good mystery?'

'A fantastic one.'

He winks and my throat is dry suddenly.

Keep it light. Keep it fun.

I reach up and lace my fingers behind his head, pulling him down, greedily seeking his mouth, taking everything he offers and still demanding more. There is nothing light about this, even while it is the most fun I've ever had.

My need for him—and I'm not blind or stupid enough to pretend I *don't* need him—is all-consuming. If I'm not careful it is going to take over, and I will no longer have autonomy.

I have to fuck him and go.

I push him angrily, needily, desperately, and together we roll off the couch onto the carpeted floor. He laughs, but I'm ripping the condom out of his hands and tearing it open, sliding it from its packet and pushing it onto him. His eyes are watching me, and it makes my fingers shake. I remove my own underwear quickly, then straddle him, leaning forward to kiss him at the same time I take him deep inside me.

Passion tears through us and we are fast, we are hungry, we are desperate. I move my hips, but he makes a growl of frustration and rolls us so that he is on top of me, the weight of his body a heavenly pleasure. I wrap my legs around his waist but he catches my calves and lifts them higher. I can't contain the furious pleasure that is taking over me. I lie back, my eyes squeezed shut as flames lick my nerves, making me tremble and sweat.

He stills and I groan, twisting my hips.

'Look at me.'

The command is husky, and he accompanies it with fingers that press under my chin, pulling my face towards him, angling me so that I am facing him.

'Look at me,' he says again, and I realise my eyes are still squeezed shut.

I blink them open and regret it immediately. It is as though I have been stabbed. Something unpleasant and sharp thrusts into my chest—something I don't recognise yet but know I don't want. I look over his shoulder but he shakes his head.

'I want to see you come.'

'You will,' I whisper, knowing that the wave is about to crash. Any minute.

He pushes deeper and I draw in an unsteady breath, digging my fingernails into my palms.

'Let me see you.'

I don't know what he means. I look to him for clarification and our eyes lock. He moves inside me, not looking away, and I don't look away either because suddenly I can't. There are invisible forces at work and they compel me to be brave even when I'm running from this feeling.

This perfect, perfect torment.

Inexplicably, tears threaten to moisten my eyes. I blink, but still I look at him. And I fall. I fall off the edge. There is nothing to hold, nothing to save my fall. I am weightless in the air—just me, my pleasure, no gravity, nothing.

I'm sure he sees this, because he's watching me so closely, and because he kisses me differently as I tremble in his arms. A kiss of warmth rather than heat. Of understanding and acceptance. I kiss him back.

What else can I do?

He moves inside me slowly, letting muscles that are squeezing him frantically return to their normal state, and then he thrusts hard, so that I cry out, and we are falling together this time, holding hands, riding the same wave of pleasure at the same time. I cry his name into his mouth over and over again. Not Ethan Ash, because he is just Ethan again. Ethan who makes me feel as I never knew I could.

Ethan who is mine. Not the world's.

Though he is. I know that.

But like this, right here, he is mine.

And I am his.

The thought rattles through me as though I am an empty barn and it is tumbleweed. It rocks me to my core.

I am no one's.

I stiffen beneath him and press my fingers into his chest. I angle my head away.

'You are fucking amazing,' he says. '*This* is amazing.'

'It's not me,' I say seriously.

'I think it must be.'

He kisses the tip of my nose and my gut twists. I must flee from this tempting perfection before it sucks me under and robs me of breath and sanity altogether.

'I should go.'

His laugh is husky. 'I'm still inside you.'

He throbs and my breath catches in my throat. Heat suffuses my cheeks.

'I know.' With great effort I make my voice light. Amused.

'You're not going anywhere.'

He pulls away from me, though, straightening and then standing, striding through the hotel room towards the bathroom. I watch him go, my eyes hungrily devouring this aspect of him—his beautiful, naked body.

He emerges a minute later, a towel wrapped low around his waist. He strides to the phone and picks it up. 'Ethan Ash. Give me Room Service.'

I prop myself on my elbows, knowing I should make an effort to get dressed, but enjoying watching him too much. I'll move soon, I tell myself.

He turns to face me; our eyes lock. I am lost once more. I can feel him inside me even though he is across the room. The phantom of his being with me is a powerful, beautiful thing.

'Fillet steak. Fries. Onion rings. A salad.' He lifts a brow questioningly and covers the receiver. 'Anything else?'

I shake my head.

'Ice cream. Some oysters. Maybe some garlic bread. A peach.'

He winks at me, then hangs up as he strides over to me. He stares at me for a heart-thumping second, his expression unreadable, and then he drops his hands down, inviting me to grab them.

I know it's not wise, but I put my hands in his as if on autopilot and he pulls me up to stand. Our bodies press to one another. My breath catches.

'I've missed you.'

My heart drops.

He can't have missed me. It's not what we are.

I smile, but I know it's only half a smile. I'm too perturbed, confused, concerned, to be properly amused.

'I want to ask you something.'

I don't think my look is encouraging, but apparently he doesn't notice. He begins to sing again. His latest song. The one that is on all the radio stations—everywhere. His latest song that is a number one hit.

God, he's so famous.

And yet we speak as though it doesn't matter.

'Yeah?' It's a hoarse prompt.

'I'm doing a gig Friday night. Wanna come?'

It takes several seconds for me to connect the words with the truth. The fact that by 'doing a gig' he means performing at a concert. And not a little local town hall concert either.

'Where?' I ask with a sinking heart.

'The Garden.'

'Madison Square Garden?'

He nods.

He'll be performing for tens of thousands of people. On Friday night. When I would usually be at happy hour with my two best friends.

'That's okay,' I say, not quite sure how to reply properly. 'I'm good.'

'I *know* you're good,' he responds with a wry twist of his lips. 'I'm asking if you want to come to the concert.'

I bite down on my lip and decide honesty is the best policy. 'Will you be offended if I say no?'

He laughs. 'No. My ego isn't *that* fragile. I'm curious, though.'

Naturally. 'It's just…' How can I put into words what I don't fully understand myself?

'You don't like my music?' he teases.

'Can't stand it,' I quip back.

His smile makes my stomach lurch. 'I just…'

'Yes?'

His lips are twitching at the corners, showing his amusement even as he tries to listen seriously to whatever wisdom I'm about to share.

'I don't know. I mean… I just… First of all, I don't see you like that. I know you're some superstar, but I like it that this feels so normal.' I pause. 'I mean apart from the luxurious apartment, the mega-mansion at the heart of the village and your penchant for ordering everything off the room service menu.'

He laughs.

'And we both know this isn't a relationship.' I force myself to meet his eyes. 'We're two people who have agreed to…to sleep together. To fuck. That's our thing.' I sigh. 'I had fun today. At the MoMA with you. But we shouldn't do that again.'

'We can do the Staten Island Ferry next time,' he teases.

'I'm serious, Ethan.' I need him to understand. 'We've both said what we want from this. The MoMA, your concert… Those things aren't on my list.'

He stares at me long and hard for a few seconds. 'I thought we said we'd have fun?'

'Yeah. *Sexy* fun.'

He laughs. 'I found you *very* sexy at the MoMA. Think of it as foreplay, baby. It was just one afternoon.'

'No.' I shake my head quickly. 'It's more complicated than that.'

His eyes crinkle at the corners, as if he's trying really hard not to laugh. 'Has anyone ever told you that you have a tendency to overthink shit?'

'Not so eloquently,' I mumble.

His laugh is short. 'Well, you do.'

'There's danger in this,' I say seriously, softly, pulling him back to the heart of my worries. 'Danger for *me*.'

His eyes throb with mine. He is reading me. Studying me. Analysing me. I keep my expression blank of emotion with an enormous effort.

'Who hurt you?'

The question knocks me sideways. I drop his hand and take a step backwards.

'No one.'

I move towards the window. I'm awkward. My body is hot and cold.

'Who hurt you?'

'No one.' I say it more emphatically now. 'You think that the only reason a person can not want to be in a relationship with you is that she's running from a past trauma, or something? Talk about egomaniacal.'

The charge is completely unreasonable—particularly given that he's right.

'I think there's more to this than you're telling me,' he insists quietly.

My eyes lift to his in the reflection of the window. There is strength in his stance and I feel it push against me. I suck in a breath; it barely reaches my lungs.

'So?' I'm on the defensive. I make a point to lower my voice. 'Have you told me everything about you and Sienna?'

I see his frown in the reflection. 'No.'

'But you think I should be an open book to *you*?'

'Hey.'

He walks behind me slowly, but his hands on my shoulders are firm. Demanding. He turns me around, then presses his thumb beneath my chin, holding my face towards his.

'You're the one who's acting like I've just fucking proposed. Why?'

'I'm not.' I bite down on my lip and jerk away from him. 'I just don't want you to go shifting the goalposts.'

I sink my teeth into my lip harder. His eyes drop to the gesture.

My heart twists painfully. Far worse than his desire to negotiate our...whatever this is...is his quick acceptance of my position. I know it's for the best, but it hurts that he doesn't fight harder.

What am I wanting? Him to prove that he wants more from me than I'm willing to give? What kind of emotional sadist am I becoming?

'So, a concert, huh?' I say, the words so overbright they are brittle, like wood that's been left in the sun for days on end. Paint peels away my confidence. 'You nervous?'

His own smile is dismissive, distracted. 'No. It's not my first time.'

'No, of course.'

We're on safer ground, and I'm grateful, but the awkwardness of our conversation is still between us, lumpy and insistent. I hate it. I hate it that we've argued. I hate it that he probably thinks I'm either completely crazy or completely weird.

'You've been doing this a long time, I guess?'

He sighs. Wearily.

Weary of me?

Warning bells flash.

I'm messing everything up.

Isn't that the point? Isn't that why I'm fighting to keep my emotions out of this?

'Yeah.'

I sidestep his touch. Our intimacy is gone. We're just two strangers in a cold room full of misunderstanding. My dress is by the door. I move towards it on legs that are shaking, lift it up with the tips of my fingers and pull it on. When I turn around he's watching me, with that same look of confusion on his handsome face.

God, he deserves better than this.

I swallow, looking towards the window, uneasy and uncertain.

'You're not wrong.'

The words are so soft they're almost a whisper; I don't even realise I'm going to say them until I hear the way they float across the room towards him.

'About what?'

I clear my throat. 'Before you, I hadn't... It had been a while since I'd been with anyone else.'

'But there was someone important before me?' he prompts.

I nod, my eyes locking to his, showing the depth of my emotion and the ache of my pain. 'Yes.'

'And it didn't work out?'

He says it gently, like teasing a knot out of a rope.

I shake my head and those stupid, *stupid* tears are back, hot in my eyes. I blink furiously, wiping them away without touching my face.

'What happened?'

He asks the question with such kindness that I think I could collapse.

I don't.

I'm not going to be weakened by Jeremy any more. I'm stronger now. Stronger than when I first met him and I believed in fairy tales and happily-ever-after and soulmates. *What a load of nonsense.*

Ethan takes my silence for an unwillingness to discuss it.

'Look…' He shifts his weight from one foot to the other. 'You don't have to talk about it. But don't run away from me, Alicia. Just…stay and have more fun.'

My body jerks at the prospect. It's what I need and want. More than anything.

'Why don't you have a bath? Relax. I'll call you when dinner gets here.'

He's being so kind and it's hurting my heart to experience that, knowing the limitations of what we are.

I nod, though, and move towards the enormous bathroom before he can see the emotions on my face. And before I can make sense of them.

Because they're scaring me half to death.

We have devoured almost the whole tray of room service food. Despite the fact I said I wasn't hungry, it turns out that incredible, mind-blowing, multiple orgasm sex is enough to give anyone an appetite.

'Things with me and Sienna hadn't been working for a long time…'

I am torn. Morbid curiosity is at the forefront of my mind, but so too is the knowledge that this discussion is dangerous.

'Why not?'

Curiosity, apparently, wins.

He reaches for a chip and eats it thoughtfully. 'I don't know.' His smile is disarming. 'Maybe we were never right together. But, man, we hated each other by the end. Still, for her to be engaged to someone else months later...'

I wince at his description and again I think of Jeremy. Of that afternoon.

'Is this what you do? You farm me off to my mother's, with our kids, so you can screw her?'

'Come on, Fiona! Why wouldn't I be fucking around behind your back? You're as cold as ice and I'm bored. We never see each other any more. I don't remember the last time we actually fucked.'

The memory makes my heart hurt.

'I guess relationships change. People change. Love is complicated,' I say with a shrug. 'Do you know the guy?'

'Tom Banks?' He grimaces. 'Yeah.'

'That's so much worse,' I say softly. 'Do you like him?'

Ethan shrugs. 'The thing is, I kind of thought something was going on between them. She told me I was imagining it.'

My stomach twists. Lies. Love and lies. How common—and complex—it is.

'How long were you guys together?'

'On and off around six years,' he says.

As though that's nothing. As though that doesn't change everything. Honestly, if he'd told me they'd had twins together I'd have been less shocked.

That's a hell of a long time. He's only twenty-eight. So they started dating when he was in his early twenties. I blink at him, but he doesn't seem to realise how spun out I am.

'We were friends for another six or so years before that.'

It's Jeremy and Fiona all over again. A shiver runs down my spine—that same trickling sense of being an outsider, running over me like a rash. But for some reason this almost seems worse, and I can't say why.

'All this…the fame thing…it's a tricky son of a bitch. I guess because I knew Sienna *before*. Before I made it…before she made it… I thought that somehow future-proofed us. I thought that made us more real.'

Does he know how hard this is to hear? Of course not. I've told him I want nothing from him. So we're people who fuck…and apparently now I'm his therapist as well.

I'm tempted to establish some kind of barrier here. A line in the sand meaning we don't talk about Sienna *or* Jeremy. But my morbid curiosity is still thick inside me and I find it impossible to ignore.

'Do you miss her?'

His eyes latch to mine and his smile spreads across his face slowly. But there is resignation in that look, too. 'I seem to have found the perfect Band-Aid.'

CHAPTER TEN

'LOOKING FOR SOMEONE?'

I tweak the E-string, play a chord, closing my eyes as I find every single note. They are floating through space and I am able to see them from every angle—but, more than that, they reverberate in my blood, hitting a frequency that I know intimately.

Then I hear the question. Carl has toured with me for years; he knows me well. In that moment, I think he knows me better than I would like.

'Nah.'

It's a lie. I keep wondering if she'll come. Thinking how annoying it is that she hasn't.

Why does it piss me off so much? Hard to say.

'Sienna here?'

Sienna? Is that who he thinks I'm scouring the audience for? 'Nah. We broke up, remember?'

'Fuck. Sorry, mate.'

I grimace, turning back to the guitar. I play the beginning of 'Wild Silver', sing a few lines into the mic and then stop abruptly. I wrote this song for Sienna. *With* Sienna. The memory is like a ball, bobbing on the horizon of a stormy ocean. I can see it, but it keeps fading away and there's no way I can reach it.

How many of my memories will be like this? Inextricably linked to her but no longer tangible?

'Did you hear about the tickets?'

I blink, focusing my attention back on Carl. On the now. Only there's a different mirage on the horizon now. One that makes me smile rather than frown.

If Ally's not here, where *is* she?

I picture her naked in my suite. In the shower, lathered up, slippery and sweet, singing in that sweet off-key way she has. All of me is pulled. I want to be with her. Fuck the concert.

'Nah. What about them?'

'Someone's scalping seats for a thousand bucks.'

I arch a brow, yet I'm not totally surprised. The concert was booked out in under thirty minutes. My management refused a second show.

'Jesus...'

'Yeah.'

Carl hands me another of my guitars. I pass the Fender over and begin to tune the Gibson.

'You all good for drinks after?'

Shit. I'd forgotten about that. Our tradition. I always take the crew out for a post-concert winddown.

But... *Ally.* Naked in my shower. In my bed.

I'm saved from needing to answer by the arrival of Grayson and my manager, Paul. I smile at them, but in my mind I'm already back at the hotel, and Ally's eating out of the palm of my hand...

* * *

I tell myself I made the right decision. I'm not a
groupie and I think it would be weird to see Ethan
up on stage, larger than life, as Ethan Rock God Ash.

So why am I sitting glued to my phone, stalking
the Twitter hashtag *#ethanashNYC*? Which is trending—of course.

There are videos of the concert being uploaded
and I watch them almost faster than they can appear.

There's his beautiful acoustic cover of 'Hallelujah,' which sends goosebumps into every part of my
body, like shooting stars chasing their natural end.
Then there are his faster, earlier songs, full of youth
and enthusiasm. There's a few ballads. He performs
a song with Hunter Smith and Esther Scott, of Scott
Smith—only my favourite band *ever*.

He looks amazing.

I mean, *amazing*.

And like himself as well.

Only it's so hard to reconcile Ethan—*my* Ethan—
with this guy. This guy who's performing in front of
tens of thousands of screaming fans. Women who
are passing out. Who are shouting his name, waving
their hands, holding posters that cry out their love for
him. And he's so…*cool*. So effortless. He waves. He
sings. He wanders from one side of the stage to the
other, sauntering with his trademark nonchalance,
and my pulse is raging.

My God.

He is so hot.

And he is mine.

Shh! I silence the grumpy part of my mind that constantly wants to remind me not to get too possessive or invested.

I seem to have found the perfect Band-Aid.

Those words have chased themselves around my head, and finally I can admit that they spark relief in me. They free me. Because they show me that he is indeed using me as a crutch. On the rebound while he gets over Sienna. And that means I can relax. This isn't serious for him.

Which means this is okay.

It's okay that I am waiting for him.

That I am in his hotel room and that he knows I am here, that he has promised to hurry back. That he told me he'd be counting the minutes.

Because I'm just a Band-Aid. And he's just hot sex. It's simple. Easy. I'm in control. Our boundaries are established and we are staying firmly within them.

Anticipation rolls through me. I look around his suite, checking all the details with a small smile. Candles. Music. Dinner.

Me in a slinky black negligee and nothing underneath.

I curl up on the sofa, dragging my finger down my phone obsessively, refreshing my feed as though my life depends on it.

And finally the concert is over.

It can't be long now, right?

How long?

I stare at my phone, contemplate messaging him

but decide not to. *I* know that I'm desperate to see him; *he* doesn't need to.

It's almost an hour later when I hear noises outside the hotel room. And with the moment upon me I am nervous suddenly! I stand up uneasily, running my hands down the front of my lingerie, my eyes fixed to the door. I fan my hair from my face quickly, just to give it body, and then I wait.

Seconds.

Just seconds.

But long enough for my heart to flutter and my stomach to twist and my brow to sweat and my mouth to dry out.

I wait, and I stare, and finally he pushes the door inwards.

I'm not sure what I'm expecting. For him to step inside, shut the door, and look around?

He doesn't. He opens the door and looks right at me. As though he knew exactly where I'd be, exactly how I'd be standing, waiting. Our eyes lock and time ceases to exist. There is a void. A black hole with just us at its cosmic heart.

Who moves first? I can't say. I know only that we are both moving, and we are both urgent, our arms wrapping around one another, our mouths seeking, our bodies melding. His shirt is wet with perspiration. I wrap my arms around him and seek his mouth. I kiss him and he kisses me, pushing me through the room while his hands roam my back.

I grip his shirt, lifting it, finding his beautiful flesh, his chest, and I drop kisses along the ridge of his neck, down to his pecs. I taste his salty perfection and he laughs, lifting his hands to my wrists and holding me still, holding me back.

My eyes fly to his; hunger must be visible in them. It is almost burning me alive.

'Not like this.'

'Like what?'

'I need to shower. I'm all sweaty.'

I laugh. 'I don't care.' I push his pants down, finding his ass and cupping it in the palms of my hands.

He swears, fisting my hair and pressing his forehead to mine. His eyes are shut, his face scrunched up.

'*Fuck*, Alicia.'

'Shower later.'

I tilt my head, chasing his lips with mine, kissing him, inviting him. Begging him. I drag my mouth lower, nipping his shoulder with my teeth, laughing when he growls in reply.

'Fuck me now.'

I bite him again and he makes a guttural noise.

He acquiesces, stepping backwards, pulling me with him, so that we are kissing, walking in a tangle of limbs and lust and discarded clothes towards the bedroom.

'This is nice,' he grunts, pushing my negligee down, sliding it over my body quickly, desperately. The silk slides across my skin like liquid as it reaches my hips and then falls to the floor. I step out of it at the same time as he pulls me to the bed.

He is on top of me and I don't question it. I don't

question the fact that he is making love to me and I
am not in control. I don't question the fact that I'm
staring up at him, my heart thumping, my body alive
with needs that only he can address.

He remembers protection—thank God. It's nowhere near my mind. He slides it down his cock and
then his hands are on my inner thighs, separating my
legs, his eyes hooked to mine as he pushes into me.

The ownership is immediate and intense.

He is just Ethan. *My* Ethan. And he is fucking
fantastic.

But tonight he is also Ethan Ash, superstar rock
god, and I am his.

I press my fingers into his hips and he rolls low,
reaching deep inside me. His fingers run over my
bare chest, finding my breasts, holding them, cupping them, and his fingers flick my nipples. I cry
out; he smiles.

He drops his mouth, taking one with his tongue,
kissing it, rolling it, teasing it. I am panting with
pleasure just beyond my reach. He thrusts hard at the
same time as his mouth clamps down on my nipple
and I am done. I cry out as I begin to fall apart and
yet he doesn't stop. Even as my body explodes at its
zenith of ecstasy he is driving me to new heights of
awareness and need, to new pleasures and sensations.

I dig my heels into the bed and push up, keeping us close, connected, making sure he stays right
where I need him. But Ethan is the master of my
body. He knows without being told. He is still when

I need him to be, knowing that I'm at my limit, and he watches me.

I watch him back.

He does not need to ask me to look into his eyes this time. I cannot look away. I don't want to. I am helpless, though. In the depths of his eyes there is something that calls to me, and I answer it without even knowing what it is.

I answer it with *all* of me. Every single piece of me is like a puzzle and it slides into place.

He thrusts again and I moan, riding the wave he is creating, being pulled under by it. His hands lift higher, finding my hair, and he runs his fingers through its length, worshipping it as his body owns mine.

He moves faster and brings his mouth to mine, kissing me hard, pushing my head as his hands thread through my hair and his body controls mine. I cry out into his mouth as my orgasm explodes and he answers with his own throaty oath, pushing himself into me and tipping us both over the edge. His body shakes on top of mine and I brace him with my legs, wrapping them around his waist, kissing him even as we are both disintegrating.

My heart.

My heart is all I am aware of.

It is thumping heavily, hard and fast, demanding I listen to it. I am, but I don't know what it is saying.

I know only that I have never, ever, in all my life, known the pleasure that Ethan Ash can create.

It is wrapping around me, tighter than rope, holding me prisoner, making me ache and fly all at the same time.

He shifts a little. Our eyes lock. I smile.

All of me smiles.

From the inside out.

'Hi.'

'Hey.' It's a gravelled admission.

'How was your concert?'

His eyes roam my face with a lazy interest that turns me on in different ways. His confidence is a thing of beauty, because it is natural and so different from egotism. I have learned the difference—before Jeremy I thought they were one and the same thing.

'Good.'

'You've taken over the Twitterverse.'

He arches a thick, dark brow. 'Yeah?'

'Uh-huh. You're a top-trending hashtag.'

His face flashes with something I don't recognise. 'That's normal.'

I laugh. 'For *you*, maybe.'

'For anyone performing at the Garden.'

His finger finds my breast and he traces a circle around my nipple, making my breath husky. I watch him watch me and my hunger intensifies. My need for him is unending.

'Tell me something…' I murmur.

'Something.'

His grin flips my stomach.

My smile is just a whisper on my lips. He swaps his hand to my other breast and I breathe in sharply.

'You were saying…?' he prompts.

'I forget.'

He laughs and removes his hand. I make a noise of complaint and reach for his wrist, dragging him back. I like it when he touches me. No, I love it. I love *everything* about being with him.

Wait. Where the hell did *that* come from?

I love *fucking* him. That's it.

Goosebumps run over my flesh.

I flip up onto my side but he keeps his hand where it is. For a moment. Then he drags it down my side, resting it on my hip. For a moment. Before yanking me closer, so our bodies are touching. I feel his hardness against me and my eyes flicker half-shut.

'If you hadn't become a world-famous super-star—'

'As opposed to one of the non-famous superstars?' he interrupts with a lazy grin.

'Right.' I nod importantly. 'If you hadn't become a world-famous, super-interrupting superstar, what would you have been?'

'A gigolo?'

I giggle. 'I'm serious.'

'Right.'

He moves his hand again, curling it around my ass, his fingers drumming against my flesh, stirring new heat.

'The thing is, Ally…'

God, the way he says my name is *so* amazing.

'It's not about the fame. That's incidental. If I'd only been able to be a busk on a corner, playing my songs, I'd have done that. It's always been about the music.'

His passion—oh, how can I *not* respond to his passion? It is *so* sexy.

He leans over and kisses me, his fingers still pressing against my ass, our naked bodies hard against one another. But he separates from me suddenly and without warning, so the impact is intense and immediate.

'I'm going to grab a quick shower.'

He stands, sexy and naked, and I watch him disappear through the door, sauntering through the lounge area of the suite. He bends and reaches for his jeans, lifting his phone out of the pocket.

He does something with it. I watch curiously. But it is the work of a moment. A quick text? A check on Twitter? Whatever... He is gone again, and a second later I hear the shower running.

I push back against the bed, breathing in the smell of him that still hangs in the air.

My fingertips run over my body without my knowledge, touching the skin that he has sensitised, that his lips have kissed, that his body has possessed.

I listen to the shower and impatience zips through me.

Impatience to see him again.

I push up, my body sore in the best possible way, and stroll through the hotel room. I pick up our clothes as I go, used to this now. Used to removing the signs of our passion almost as quickly as they appeared. I lay his jeans over the back of the sofa and place my negligee on top, then pad naked into the bathroom.

He's humming, his body covered in shower gel foam, hot water steaming the glass, so that I see him without seeing all the glorious details of his body.

Hungrily, I move closer, listening, smiling, admiring.

His eyes are shut, and I can just make out his spiky lashes, all clumped and wet.

'Hi.' I prop my hip against the vanity unit, my smile widening as he opens his eyes and looks towards me.

'Hey...'

'Don't stop.'

He arches a brow. 'If you wanted to hear me sing you should have come tonight.'

'Didn't I just come?' I tease.

He laughs, but starts singing again—louder, so beautiful. His voice is like warm caramel and sunshine, but it's dusty too, with a depth and husk that makes my knees weak. There is no one like him. He channels the best of Bruno Mars, Ed Sheeran, Jason Mraz, and yet he is singularly unique.

'I could listen to you sing all day.'

He pushes the glass shower door open and holds a hand out without breaking off the song. *Thank God.* I step in and he pulls me close, moving his hips as he sings. I can see the passion on his face. A passion for music. He creates worlds with his voice—the same way I do when I put pieces of art together. When I create a room. A feeling. A mood.

He sings on, holding me close. He's looking straight a but I know that he's seeing the song, feeling the words. It is beautiful, magical. Water streams over us. I don't want to say or do anything that will break the moment. I watch him closely and my heart thumps hard against my ribs, my stomach swirls.

At the end of the song I lift up on tiptoes and kiss him.

Gently.

Gratefully.

His music is a gift and he gave that song to me.

Just me.

It is so much more special than if I'd seen him at the concert.

'Now, why would I go stand with a heap of screaming fans when I get to listen to you in the shower?'

His grin is beautiful. 'The acoustics in here are actually pretty fantastic.'

'I'll say…'

His fingers wander over my skin, and I sigh.

'Okay, Ethan Ash. Dinner's ready.'

He groans, rolling his hips. 'But it's so *good* in here…'

He's right. Being in the shower with him, I am in a blissed-out state of nirvana. I cup his cheeks.

'That's true.' I reach behind him and flick the taps off. 'But I've cooked, and I never do that, so you kind of *have* to eat it.'

'You've *cooked*?' He's fascinated by that. *'Where?'*

'At my place.'

He's frowning. Thinking. Instinctively I shy away from his thoughts, despite having no clue what they are.

'You live with those two women?'

'Eliza and Cassie? Yeah.'

'How'd you meet them?'

I step out of the shower and he's right behind me. He reaches for a towel and hands it to me. I know it's a small, inconsequential gesture, but there's something in the tiny little act of thoughtfulness that pokes holes in my resolution to keep him at arm's length.

I harden my heart as I dry my arms. Easier said than done. Because he's watching me, smiling.

And then he sings again. Only it's a song with my name in it.

Hair like flame, I turn to fire
Sky-blue eyes, you're my bad liar
Can't hide secrets you try to keep
Truth seems to make you weep, Ally... Ally...

My smile is heavy. As if resin has been poured over my face, casting me in a mask that will be an approximation of how I really look for ever.

'Is that about me?'

'Nah.' He reaches for a second towel and rubs it through his hair. 'It's for another girl I know. Alisandre.'

I roll my eyes. '*You're* the bad liar.'

He laughs. 'I don't think so.'

I wrap the towel around me, tucking it under my

arms. The song echoes through me. 'What do you think I'm lying about?'

'It's lyrical,' he says with a shrug, but then he looks at me curiously, his expression watchful. 'I don't think you're lying. I think you're...closed off.'

'Closed off?' I arch my brows and think my expression must show how unimpressed I am. 'Seriously? I have been more intimate with you than... than anyone in a really long time.'

'*That*. Right there. *That's* what you do. You catch yourself before you can say *anything* about yourself.'

'That's not true!'

'Okay. Why do you love that painting at the MoMA so much?'

My cheeks flush pink. 'I told you...'

'You *"just do".*' He imitates my voice and rolls his eyes, but his lips are twitching into a smile. 'See? Vague, vague, vague.'

'Well, no... I just...' I huff an indignant breath. 'It's kind of embarrassing.'

'Yeah?'

He crosses his arms over his naked chest and my eyes drop lower. Man, it's so much easier when we're having sex. There are no barriers then.

I grimace at the secret I'm about to share. Something I've never told anyone.

'When I was in middle school I really hated the way I looked. You know—bright white skin, orange hair...'

'It's not orange,' he murmurs.

'It felt like it. Everyone else was blonde and tanned

and I was all...*me*.' I shrug. 'My mom wouldn't let me dye my hair, even though I desperately wanted highlights.' I sigh dramatically. 'And then I saw that painting. And...and she was so beautiful and mysterious and she kind of looked like me. Don't you think?'

'No one looks like you,' he says, wrapping his arms around me.

His voice is thick and so full of sincerity that it reaches right into my heart and curls around it.

'You are completely unique.'

The atmosphere between us is a net, tangling me in its midst. I stare at him, and everything is quiet but the beating of my heart and the gushing of the super-charged blood through my veins.

It's too much.

I smile awkwardly and step away from him, moving out of the bathroom, my heart still racing, my body aching for him.

'So...' He follows me, all casual nonchalance because he knows it's what I need. 'What'd you cook?'

'Ah!' Safer ground. 'Lasagne.'

'My favourite.'

I'm rewarded with a grin. A grin that curls my toes.

Apparently *not* safer ground.

I move on to business, seeking something that will suck the sparkle out of the air around us.

The lasagne is burned on top.

It almost does the trick.

His kisses run like raindrops down my skin. They are soft and sweet and I shift a little.

'Was I asleep?' I stretch in the bed, lifting a hand to capture his cheek. My heart twists.

'Yeah. Did I wake you?'

'Uh-huh.' I blink. My mind is groggy. 'What time is it?'

'Four.'

'Four a.m.?'

I frown. *Shit.* I planned to go after we'd eaten. Why am I still here?

'Why are you awake?'

He lifts his mouth higher, finding my breast and kissing the underside before reaching a nipple and wrapping his lips around it. It is bliss, but too short. He moves higher, pressing his lips against a pulse point at the base of my throat, and then he samples my lips.

But it's a kiss that lacks our usual desperation and urgency. I am tired and he is probing me. Curiosity is at the fore of this exploration.

I sigh softly.

'I never sleep after a concert.'

'Really?' I lift a hand up and stroke his hair. 'Why not?'

He shrugs. 'Too wired.'

'Let me teach you a trick.'

'What is it?'

'Lie down.'

He does, on his back, beside me. I rearrange myself so that my head is on his chest, listening to his heart, and search for his hand, lacing our fingers together and resting them on his chest.

'What do you usually do instead?'

'Of this?'

'No. Instead of sleeping.'

'Oh.' His fingers wander over my hair distractedly. 'I go out with my crew.'

'Your crew?'

'Yeah. Like technical crew. Not gangsta.'

'But not tonight?'

His fingers still for a moment. 'No. Not tonight.'

Because of me.

The implication is so beautiful. And so problematic.

'What's the trick?'

'Oh. This. Is it not working?'

He breathes in deeply. I feel his chest move and smile.

'Kind of.' He yawns. 'How could you have ever hated your hair?' He murmurs. 'I have dreams about it.'

'My hair?'

'Yeah.'

'Really?'

'Of course. Your hair. Your body. Your smile.' He yawns again. 'Your eyes. Your body.'

'You said that one already.'

'It's worth an extra credit.'

I smile. My fingers, still held by his, stroke his chest beneath them. I touch him rhythmically, enjoying the feel of his body, the way it is so vibrant and alive, warm and smooth.

I shift a little, burrowing against him.

'Thanks for staying tonight.'

I don't respond. I don't plan to stay. It would be really, really stupid. But I'm tired, and he is asleep before I can think of the words. I don't want to risk waking him up. And besides...

There's nowhere else I'd rather be.

I can say it to myself. There's no harm in that, is there?

I am falling asleep. Ally is against me, our breath-sounds matching. We are our own music: a song of our bodies' making. I stroke her in time to the lyric-less song and it is perfect. A slice of time that belongs with the stars for its beauty.

But the stars are so far away. Beautiful, yes, but distant—and I don't want to make that comparison with Ally.

Nor do I want to think about how good she is at *this*. How right it feels.

I don't want to wonder about who else she has held so close, breathing in sync with him, helping him to fall asleep as she is me.

CHAPTER ELEVEN

IT IS LATE when I stir, and Ethan is no longer in bed. I blink, a little disorientated, a lot satisfied, and stretch my arms over my head, smothering a yawn. Then I am still. I listen. I hear music.

I push the duvet back and step out of bed, padding into the lounge. He has his back to me, sitting in the wing-back armchair, looking out of the window at Manhattan. It occurs to me that no one out there has any idea that Ethan *trending-on-Twitter* Ash is right here, high above them like some beautiful, sexy sky-angel.

I know the song he's playing. It's not his. I think it's Bob Dylan's. I listen, trying to catch the words, but he's humming them quietly, as though he's not even aware he's singing.

Is this what it's like for him? Does the need to make music simply overtake him? Beyond his control, his realisation, his intention?

Much like the way I am moving towards him, which is also beyond my intention. I have sometimes felt that there is a sort of magnetism between us. I don't really go in for all that woo-woo universal energy stuff. Or, I didn't, at least.

'Hey. Sleeping Beauty's up.'

He smiles at me at the exact moment the sun beams from behind a cloud and his face glows gold. He places the guitar down as he stands and moves towards me.

He's wearing his favourite jeans—and now, let's face it, *my* favourite jeans—low on his hips. His feet are bare. So is his chest.

And suddenly my breath is lost. My throat is dry.

He wraps his arms around my waist, pulling me to him. 'How'd you sleep?'

'I think I passed out.' I smile up at him. 'That is one comfy bed.'

'You should stay over more,' he says with a grin.

It's just a throwaway comment, yet prickles of danger flush my spine. I ignore the suggestion.

'Coffee?'

'Yeah.' He nods towards the machine. 'You don't like the idea?'

'Of coffee?' I wilfully misunderstand. 'Of course I do. I live for the stuff.'

'Of staying over.'

I meet his eyes and I know my expression holds a warning. 'Ethan…'

His phone rings, interrupting whatever the hell I had been going to say.

He shoots me a look that speaks volumes. *This isn't over.*

I gnaw at my lip, half watching as he moves across

the room and lifts his phone off the coffee table, where he left it the night before. Something crosses his face—an emotion I don't comprehend—and then he drops the phone again.

'Dodging someone?'

His eyes meet mine. He's distracted. 'No.'

I remember the message he sent the night before. Or whatever it was he did. Was it to a friend? Or another woman? Or Sienna?

Something like alarm bells sound in my mind. I have to silence them. Not care. Because it's not what we are. And he's not Jeremy.

'You were saying?'

I push a pod into thecoffee machine and wait for the light to show that it's ready to wor.

'I had fun last night. But I think it's really important to remember—'

'That we're just fucking,' he interrupts. Tersely.

I am irrationally emotional in the face of his obvious annoyance. 'Well, yeah. I wasn't going to put it quite so crudely. I just mean that we should remember what we're doing here.'

'Right. The *rules*.' He nods.

He is keeping a grip on his temper but I know him better than that. I know he is tense and cross.

'And what are they again?'

I force a light smile. 'Fun! No-strings!'

'Right. And we can't do that if you stay over with me?'

'*You're* the one who said no sleepovers.'

He laughs—a harsh sound of disbelief—then

drags his fingers through his hair. Of all the tools in his arsenal, this and this alone has the power to weaken the last threads of my resolve. He looks impossibly, edibly hot, his chest rippling, his hair spiking, and yet there is such an air of sweet helplessness in the gesture that I ache to go to him and properly explain. To tell him everything.

His eyes lock to mine and it's almost as though I have.

'Who hurt you?'

The machine whirls into life, pushing coffee through with its reliable hum. I drop my attention to it, pretending fascination with the dark brown liquid that is running into the bone-china cup. But my chest is moving too fast as each breath struggles for release.

'Alicia?'

God. Hearing my full name is such a weakness. When he says it I melt.

'I…'

He thrusts his hands on his hips, staring at me, and I blink my eyes shut.

'This isn't a request for state secrets. It's not that hard.'

I bite down on my lip. 'Yeah, it is.'

I swallow and force myself to look at him. I see the interest. The speculation. The sympathy.

'It was serious with you and him?'

My nod is barely a tick. A slow lift of my head. Yet it's all the confirmation he needs.

'Yeah. We were… It was.'

'And it ended badly?'

I nod again.

He moves towards me and runs his thumb over my cheek. 'What kind of asshole would ever hurt you?'

My heart jumps. My body throbs. I don't know what to say.

'*I'm* not going to hurt you.'

'God! Don't do that, please.' I pull away from him. 'Don't be so perfect. We both know you *will* hurt me, unless I'm very careful. Don't…don't make promises you can't keep.'

'I'm not.'

'We both agreed. We want the same thing here.'

'And what if that's changing?'

'*No.*' My denial is sharp, and panic is obvious in my voice. 'It can't.'

'Why not?'

'For many, many reasons.'

'Such as?'

'Well… You're not in any kind of place to be getting serious with anyone. And I've just… I've done that. I've done the whole falling in love thing. Getting to know someone. Swapping secrets. Planning a future.'

My voice cracks and I think of my engagement ring for the first time in months. Unconsciously I rub my finger, trying to focus my thoughts. Ethan is watching me, though, and I am distracted by him.

'I'm not… I'm barely myself again. *Eight months.*' My eyes feel hollowed out. 'For eight months I have tried to make sense of how terribly things went wrong. I have tried to move on. To forget. To look in the mirror and see myself as someone other than *that* woman. It almost killed me when it ended.'

I stare at him, willing him to understand.

'I'm still so…so broken. *So* broken. If I let myself… If I let you in and you hurt me… God, Ethan. I wouldn't do so well.'

He pulls me close roughly, urgently, and he wraps his arms around me so tight, as though he can put me back together again.

'I'm not going to hurt you.'

'That's exactly what *he* would have said.'

He doesn't let go. And I really, *really* don't want him to.

'Okay,' he murmurs against my hair. 'I promise I'm not going to push this. We can do it your way.'

Relief—or I think that's what it is—moves through me.

'I'm not going to hurt you,' he says again. 'But I want to see more of you. I want to see as much of you as I can before I go.'

Hurt. Pain. It lashes through me.

Just contemplating his absence from my life, the finality of his departure, fills me with an ache I didn't to expect.

And I know then that we have to shift the rules slightly. Because I don't want him to go from my life and for me to realise I didn't see as much of him as I could. I want to grab him with both hands while I have him, so long as my heart isn't in play.

I nod slowly. 'More is fine. Just so long as we both remember what we want here.'

'You know what *I* want?' he says seriously, his expression impossible to interpret.

'What's that?'

'I want a burger.'

'A burger?' I think for a second I've misheard.

'Yeah.' A sexy grin. 'A burger. Whaddya say, Miss Douglas? Brave the streets of New York with me once more?'

I have become used to indecision. I think one thing and want another. And then I question what I want and what I think until they become tangled together. But I am glad for this change in conversation topic and tempo. It is a relief not to be thinking about defining what we are, nor the rules we have already agreed *do* define us. I try not to think of them as limiting us, because that has negative connotations and our boundaries are definitely a *good* thing.

'A burger sounds good.'

It does. My stomach is prepared to answer that question.

'I know just the place. How quickly can you get ready?'

The promise of food motivates me.

I shower in record time, pulling on what I arrived in the day before—a pair of jeans and an oversized shirt. I have just a few cosmetic basics in my handbag. I wipe some concealer underneath my eyes and some rouge on my cheeks, tap a little gloss over my lips. But I've forgotten a hairbrush, meaning my hair is wild and sex-styled. I comb it with my fingers and pull it over one shoulder.

He whistles when I step out of the bathroom, low and soft, but it makes my tummy flip-flop.

'Same to you.'

He's wearing jeans and a black shirt, with the sleeves rolled up to the elbows. He's got a black baseball cap on his head. *Groan*. He's *hot*.

He puts a hand in the small of my back as we leave the hotel. The contact is nice. No, it's better than nice.

The elevator doors swish open and we move inside, but the second we're in he pushes me against the back wall and kisses me, his mouth on mine demanding. It is a kiss that drugs me with its intensity and changes the parameters of my existence.

He doesn't break it until the elevator touches down with a gentle thud on the ground floor of the hotel.

'Wait a sec.'

I am not even sure my legs can carry me, so it's easy to do as he suggests. He lifts a spare baseball cap off his head—I didn't even realise he was carrying it—and places it on mine, then reaches for my hand, pulling me out of the lift.

The foyer is as usual. There are a couple of guards by the doors. But when we step out it's like the whole world erupts.

Flashes go off in my face and Ethan, beside me, swears. He squeezes my hand and suddenly Grayson is there, pushing people back, cutting a path for us through the crowds. But they move with us, following, and I am afraid.

Beside me, Ethan tosses a look over his shoulder. 'Wankers.'

There's a car waiting. Grayson shepherds us into it. Ethan steps back to let me in first and I don't hesitate. I slide in, keeping my head down, grateful for the protection offered by the cap, which shields at least some of my face.

My breath is fierce.

Ethan moves in beside me. He stares at me for a long second and then shakes his head.

'I'm sorry about that.'

I don't know what to say. Questions and doubts run through me. He must have known that would happen?

But I've left his hotel lots of times and not seen anything like that.

'It's the concert,' he explains, reaching for my hand again and lifting it to his lips. He presses a kiss against the racing pulse point.

I nod, but only because he seems to be waiting for me to say something. I'm full of doubts.

'That's... I can't believe you live like that.'

'Yeah.' His lips compress. 'It takes a bit of getting used to.'

'I could *never* get used to it.' I shudder in revulsion. It is yet another reason to be grateful for the fact that this is going nowhere.

'It's not all the time. In fact when I'm out on my own I can usually do most stuff. I should have checked the foyer before bringing you down. That won't happen again.'

I shrug, staring out of the window. 'It's only one more week,' I point out. 'We can keep a low profile after this.'

He doesn't say anything. What is there to say?

Grayson takes us a few blocks south and pulls up outside a diner. I've never heard of it, but when we step inside the guy behind the counter comes over and wraps Ethan in a bear hug. I stand back and watch curiously.

'How you going, mate?'

'Not bad.'

'See you lit up Manhattan last night.' The man, who's wearing chef's pants and a white T-shirt, punches Ethan jokingly on the chest. 'Surprised your head still fits through the door.'

Ethan laughs. 'Benji, this is Alicia. My cousin Benji, here, happens to make the best burgers in town.'

'Think you might be biased there.' Benji grins, but reaches across and shakes my hand. 'Though they *are* pretty damned good. Nice to meet you, Alicia.'

'Likewise.'

Benji nods towards a table at the back. 'You want coffee? Beer?'

'Coffee.' Ethan nods. 'Ally?'

'Same. Thank you.'

He nods and moves through the restaurant, talking to a waitress as he goes. Our coffee appears almost instantly and I curl my hands around the cup.

'Your cousin seems nice,' I say, with my head tilted to one side. 'This is his place?'

'Yeah.'

'It's *our* place.'

Benji is back, handing menus over. Ethan makes no effort to pick his up. I don't either.

'Your place?' I prompt, studying Ethan.

'Yeah. Ash bought it years ago. Got me in to run it.'

'Huh. So you're a restaurateur-cum-rock-star, huh? Is there no end to your talents?'

Benji laughs. 'I like her. She's got your measure.'

'She has that,' Ethan agrees.

'Okay, what'll you two have?'

'The usual,' Ethan says.

'I'll have whatever you recommend.'

'Great.'

Benji winks and moves away, leaving us alone once more.

Something heavy lodges in my chest. I can't explain it, but then I realise. Ethan is renovating a house in New York. He owns this restaurant and his cousin works here. He's not leaving in a week—not really. Not for good.

He'll be back again soon and then what?

Will he call me?

What will I say?

Would I see him again?

I stare out of the window.

Worse. What if he doesn't? What if I find out

through Twitter that he's here and he hasn't thought to get in touch?

And that second option is far more likely, isn't it?

It doesn't matter. Because this is what I want.

This is all we are.

And so long as I remember that I'll be fine. He can call. Or he can not call. It changes nothing about what we are. *Nothing.*

Hours later, back in his hotel suite, I look at him and feel myself smile. Without my consent. He's reading.

Yes. Ethan panty-melting-superstar Ash *reads*—and not just anything. It's *Les Misérables*, by Victor Hugo.

'Good book?'

He presses a finger into the page and looks up at me, his own smile crooked in response. 'It's one of my favourites.'

'Really?'

'Sure. Why not?'

'I just… I don't know.'

'Oh, I see.' He grins, putting the book down and moving closer. 'You're surprised I can actually read, right?'

'No!' I deny, my cheeks burning. 'It's just not very…rock and roll.'

'So what do you *think* I do with my spare time? Snort cocaine and trash hotel rooms?'

I wrinkle my nose. If anything, he's a complete neat freak. Oh, he's sexily dishevelled in his personal appearance, but he makes his own bed each morning and tidies up after himself.

'I don't really like the whole housekeeping thing,' he said, when I asked him about it.

'Yeah. Sleep with supermodels—that kind of thing.'

He laughs. 'How boring the reality must seem.'

I grin. 'You're not boring, Mr Ash.'

'I'm glad to hear it, Miss Douglas.'

He moves closer and so do I, drawn as ever by that inevitable pull. He smells insanely good. It is dark outside now, and his hotel room is warm. I know I will need to leave soon, get home and get ready for work the next day, but I am reluctant to bring our weekend to an end.

I should be worried by that, but I cling to our agreement and trust in my own strength. He'll go, and I'll be fine.

I ignore the strange presentiment of emptiness that fills me.

'I have a question for you.'

I lift myself up and straddle him, smiling at his immediate look of desire. At the way I feel him harden beneath me.

'I'm yours. Ask me anything.'

My laugh is soft and husky. 'Anything? Hmm… Maybe I don't want to waste that on this question.'

'You can ask me anything. Again and again.'

His generosity, sweetness and openness are beautiful.

But didn't I feel that about Jeremy?

'You're amazing. I can't believe I got so lucky as to have you in my life. Ally, marry me. Please. I want to spend every morning waking up beside you...'

God!

An acidic taste permeates my mouth. I focus on Ethan beneath me. Ethan who's holding my hands. Ethan who's pulling me into his world with no expectations or strings.

'Where does Grayson go when you're up here?'

'Grayson?' He pulls a face. 'I don't know if I want to think about him right now.'

I grin. 'Sorry. I was just wondering if he's, like, sitting outside the door, waiting for you to call.'

'He has a room on the same floor,' Ethan says after a small beat of time.

'And how does it work? If you go out you text him and he has to stop whatever he's doing...?'

'I try to give him notice if I'm changing the schedule.'

'And he's your bodyguard?'

'Yeah. Technically he's my driver, but he's ex-military, ex-cop, a martial arts expert. You wouldn't want to be on his bad side.'

'Wow. I had no idea.'

'Plus, I trust him completely. He's been with me for over seven years.'

'He doesn't have family?'

Ethan shakes his head slowly. 'He was married once.'

'It didn't work out?'

Ethan looks over my shoulder. And despite the

fact that he said I could ask him anything I sense that he's feeling awkward about betraying his friend's trust.

I lean forward and hover my lips just above his. Close enough that I can feel his breath but not touching him. 'It doesn't matter. It's not my business.'

'It's no secret,' he murmurs, not attempting to bring himself closer.

But then he shifts his hips a little, so I feel his hard cock between my legs. Desire shreds me. How can I want him again? All we have done today is touch, kiss, feel, make love, doze, eat and repeat. Suddenly the thought of going days without being able to have him whenever I want is anathema.

All the more reason for me to get the hell out of Dodge and prove to myself that I can live without the wonder that is Ethan Ash.

'She died.'

It's ice water on my flaming needs. 'What? Who?'

'Grayson's wife. Matilda. A car crash.'

'Oh, God. That's awful.'

'Yeah. It was years ago. Before I knew him. But so far as I know he hasn't dated since.'

'That's *so* sad,' I murmur, thinking of Grayson's faithfulness to his wife.

'There's no guarantees in life, right? You just have to make the most of what you've got. Every day.'

He buzzes his lips over mine, lightly, sweetly, just so I get the faintest hint of him before he pulls away.

'Speaking of Grayson—are we going to be needing him tonight?'

I arch a brow. 'Threesomes aren't really my thing.'

'Then you're missing out,' he teases. 'I meant do we need him to take you home?'

I draw my brows together and his finger lifts to the little divot between my eyes.

'I want you to stay,' he pushes on, the words roughened, 'but I presume you're going to do your disappearing act sometime soon?'

'Right.'

I nod, but my body is screaming at me to stop being so stupid. What harm will it cause if I'm late in tomorrow? I can stay here. Spend the night in his bed and then cab it home early. It's no biggie, right?

But then what? Two nights in a row is habit-forming, and I will *not* let this become a habit. Even if Ethan Ash *is* more addictive than any substance on earth.

'I'll get a cab,' I murmur.

'Stay.' He pushes his fingers into my hair and draws my mouth to his, his kiss one of promise and pleasure.

I surrender to it on a sigh. 'A little longer.'

A little longer...

I fall into his kiss. I have been wearing a shirt of his all day. He pushes at the fabric, lifting it up, and I obligingly raise my arms, making it easier, so that I am straddling him wearing only a flimsy pair of lace panties. His mouth drops to my breasts and I cry out as his tongue rolls over the flesh that is already so sensitive. His fingers run down my back and there is something so reverential in his touch, as though

I am an object he was born to worship, that I feel a strange emotion lurch inside me.

His hands slip beneath the elastic of my underwear and he cups my ass, pulling me closer to him. I press myself down. Were it not for the barrier of clothing we would be together, and I want that.

I want everything.

It is never enough.

Should I have known that from the beginning?

Should I have understood how dangerous it is to play with fire?

Probably.

Would it have stopped me?

I doubt it.

This is as inevitable as day following night, autumn embracing winter. I want him, but I want more than that. I want to make him lose his mind as much as I am losing mine.

I pull away from him with regret, and he makes a sound of frustrated confusion. I drop to the floor between his legs and loosen his belt, my eyes holding his as I pull it from his jeans and then unclasp his button and zip.

He knows what's about to happen and he doesn't move. He stares at me, as lost in the moment as I am.

He is rock-hard and I bring my mouth to his tip first, encircling him with my tongue, my eyes locked to his as I tease him with what's to follow.

He keeps his hands by his sides, balled into fists, his expression one of determination.

'Something wrong?' I smile as I take him deeper,

rolling my tongue over him as I guide him to the back of my mouth.

'Fuck…' He shakes his head.

But as I move my mouth up and down, he moans my real name, low in his throat.

'Alicia… You are perfect.'

I'm not.

We're not.

But this is.

Our bodies might well have been forged with this in mind. They are perfectly designed to please one another. It has never been like this for me. Not with anyone before Jeremy, and not even with Jeremy.

What we shared was good once. But it was borne of love and friendship and knowing one another.

This is different.

It's indefinable.

At least for me.

I wonder if it has ever been like this for him. If it was like this with Sienna. Or anyone else. *Has* there been anyone else for him?

I know they were together a long time…

These are questions I want answered, but not now. Now I want to experience this moment to the full.

I bring one hand to cup him around his base and I roll him further back in my mouth. He lifts his hands over his head and slides lower on the sofa, giving me more access, and I taste a hint of him in my mouth.

He drops a hand to my hair, and another to my

shoulder, and I know why. He wants me to stop before he finishes.

But the power is thrilling. I take him deeper and he lets out a groan. And then he moves, sliding across the sofa, out of my grip. He moves quickly, dropping onto the floor beside me at first, and then he is behind me. He straddles me, his chest to my back, the weight of his body bending me over the sofa so that my face is flat against the cushions. He's so deep, and my body welcomes him as its master returning.

His fingers find my nipples and he teases them, pulling at them, cupping my breasts, his fingers callused against my smooth skin.

I swear low in my throat as he pushes into me again, harder, faster, and then he drops one hand to my clit and moves his fingers over me. I explode. It is fast, it is intense, and I am loud. I cry out with no care for who hears me. Pleasure rips through me like a hurricane.

I kneel straight up, arching my back, but that just gives him better access. To my breasts, to my body, and then his mouth is on my throat, kissing me as his harder-than-granite dick controls me.

I am his.

I am completely his.

'Your mouth on me is the fucking hottest thing ever.'

'No...' I shake my head, trying to find his lips. It's too awkward the way I'm positioned. '*This* is.'

He laughs—a sound of dangerous desire. He brings his hand around to my ass and then to the small of my back. He presses down with enough strength to bend me over the sofa again. I do not even dream of resisting. I am on a ride of his creation and it is a *good* ride.

The best.

He holds my hips, his fingers digging into my flesh in a way that is deliciously painful, and he drives into me, thrusting and finding every single nerve inside me. My body is melting. His fingers run over my flesh, across the curves of my ass, and I moan as he moves inside me.

Heaven is a place and it's right here—in the middle of the Gramercy Park Hotel.

It is midnight when I surface from the haze of our sensual exploration. My body is heavy with lust and liquid heat. Ethan is asleep beside me. I roll over, staring at him, watching the rhythmic intake of his breath, the gentle exhalations, and I smile at his beauty in repose. At the way he looks younger somehow. And so handsome.

I don't want to go. Which is all the more reason why I must.

I slide sideways slowly, pulling myself out from under his arm. I'm almost there. But when I'm right at the edge of the bed his fingers clamp around my upper arm and he pulls himself closer to me.

'Stay, baby,' he murmurs, the words husky and coated in sleep and dreams.

'I can't.' *I shouldn't.*

'Stay.' His eyes blink open groggily and land on my face.

And I weaken completely. I nod, smile and wriggle a little closer.

One more night won't hurt.

CHAPTER TWELVE

'IS THAT YOUR PHONE?'

I barely hear him through the haze of sleep. I am naked in his bed, my limbs heavy, my hair a tangle across my back. I push up onto my elbows and look at him quizzically, before realising that, yes, my phone is ringing.

'Oh. Sorry.' I reach for it and cringe when I see my mother's face.

I swipe it to answer at the same time as I push out of his bed, grabbing one of the hotel bathrobes and wrapping it around me, cinching it in at the waist.

'Hi, Mom.'

I move out of his bedroom and into the lounge, slipping a pod into the machine on autopilot.

'Alicia Jane Douglas. Would you mind telling me what the *hector* you're doing?'

'I'm making coffee,' I say only half-jokingly. 'Where's the outrage in that?'

'Young lady, I'm serious.'

Young lady? Uh-oh. In my mom's native tongue that's really, really serious. It sobers me.

'What about? What's happened?

"'Ethan Ash isn't wasting any time moving on from Sienna Di Giorgio after her shock engagement to Tom Banks. The Grammy award-winning star was seen leaving his hotel with the same mystery woman he was spotted out and about with in SoHo last week. Could romance be on the cards for the heartbroken singer?"'

I grab the coffee cup out of the machine and stare at it, my heart racing. 'What *is* that?'

'It's in the *papers*,' she hisses. 'I've had a photographer come to my house. This *morning*!'

Worse and worse. My mother believes calling on someone before midday is just plain rude. I grimace.

'I'm sorry, Mom. It's... It's not like it sounds.'

'Alicia, your father and I have barely recovered from your last run-in with poor decision-making. We've hardly lived down the reputation of what you did then. And now this article? Your father is the minister of this town, missy. How the hector is he going to explain *this* to his congregation?'

Colour flames my cheeks and a noise behind me alerts me to Ethan's presence.

'The same way he did last time,' I say, not caring that Ethan's there. 'What I do has nothing to do with you or him. You can say what you want. Disown me.'

'It's not that simple. You *are*, in fact, our daughter. You moved to Manhattan and assured us you wouldn't be changed by it. That you'd be the same good girl we raised. And now you're sleeping with married men and *celebrities*?'

Pain lashes through me. Because even my mother can see that being with Ethan falls into the same category of foolhardy as my relationship with Jeremy.

'It's okay, Mom. This isn't a big deal.'

'It's a big deal to *me*! *And* to your father!'

Invoking Daddy is another sign that she's seriously pissed off.

'So? Who *is* this man? Did you *really* spend the night in his hotel?'

Argh! Possibly the least comfortable conversation of my life and Ethan Ash is watching me, one shoulder propped against the doorframe, his eyes resting on me with undisguised interest.

'It's not serious,' I say slowly, and then wince.

'Not *serious*? You're giving your body to a man and it's *not serious*? Good Lord, who *are* you? I think it's time for you to come home. Spend some time with your father and me, remember how we raised you.'

'Mom...' I shake my head. 'It's okay. My immortal moral soul is not in jeopardy.'

Ethan laughs—just a soft sound, but it pulls at me. It pulls at me in a way that makes me need him. Not sexually, though. I need him to hug me.

Everything is spinning out of control—and the irony is that it's because of him yet I want *him* to fix it.

'You're laughing at me.' My mother sniffs.

'I'm not, Mom, I'm really not. But I'm twenty-five years old. I think I can be trusted to handle my own life.'

'You had an affair with a *married man*!' she exclaims, and I cringe, squeezing my eyes shut. 'You brought him home to us. You clearly *aren't* handling your life.'

'I had no way of knowing that,' I remind her softly. Her outrage hurts. The facts of my situation were all she cared about, and not the extenuating circumstances—like Jeremy's psychopathy. Nor the fact that there was no way for me to know that my 'fiancé' was a married father of two!

'I want you to come home.'

'No.' I square my shoulders. 'I know you're worried about me, Mom. But I'm fine. I'll... I'll come for Christmas, okay?'

I instantly regret the promise, but it does its job and mollifies her.

'And, please, Alicia. No more photographs in the national papers. Your daddy has a reputation to think of.'

I disconnect the call and then hurl my phone onto the sofa, wishing I could throw something else.

'Trouble?'

'Yeah!' I snap, sipping my coffee.

My fingers are shaking. With exasperation, I place the cup down on the coffee table and move towards the window, staring out at Manhattan.

'Your mom doesn't approve of me?'

'She doesn't approve of *me*,' I correct softly.

He wraps his arms around my waist and I close my eyes, leaning back against him, taking strength from his proximity, allowing myself to surrender to this.

'Because of him?'

'Jeremy.'

I say his name and it is as though I am invoking his spirit. I shiver at the fact that I've done that—that I've brought him into this room by speaking his name.

'They didn't like him?'

My lips twist in disagreement. 'Oh, they liked him fine.'

My voice is hoarse. It isn't the past I fear. It's confessing to the part I played. Guilt at what I did, even when I know that I didn't knowingly enter into an affair, colours me. I don't want Ethan to see me as I see myself.

I don't want him to know what I've done.

And yet the burden of this guilt is a weighty confession that will only be lightened by speaking.

He seems to understand. He is quiet, waiting, giving me a chance to speak.

'They thought he was a good, sensible choice.' I sigh. 'He was a banker. Educated. Wealthy. Conservative. Everything they wanted for their little girl.'

Ethan's lips buzz my cheek and a heavy smile passes over my lips.

'But it didn't work out?' he prompts after a moment.

'No.'

It's a whisper. He spins me around to face him, keeping his hands on my waist, his eyes locked to mine.

'Why not?'

I'm back in the past. 'The first time I met him I was just…just blown away.'

A muscle jerks in Ethan's jaw but I barely notice it.

'We were at an art auction and we were bidding on the same piece.' My face is shadowed with the memories I have suppressed for so long. 'I won the piece. He won the prize.' A pause. 'That's what he used to say. And you know what the worst thing is?'

'What, Ally?'

'He was trying to buy the painting for *her*.'

'Who?'

'His wife.'

The words are torn from me and I close my eyes for a long moment, not wanting to see what I know must be on his face. Judgement. Surprise. Pity.

None of those emotions are good.

'He was married?'

I nod slowly. 'I didn't know.'

'Hell, of *course* you didn't. You think I believe you'd get involved in something like that?'

His instant understanding is the last thing I expected and it's everything I need.

'You're not that kind of person.'

'I'm *not* that kind of person,' I agree urgently. 'He never told me. He didn't wear a ring. And he was so available. I mean, I saw a *lot* of him. His wife travelled a heap for work, and his kids were at her mom's a heap of the time.' I shake my head. 'It doesn't change the fact that I broke up a family…'

Ethan lifts his hands to my face, cupping it and

making me face him. 'You didn't break up a family. *He* did. And he broke your heart in the process.'

I nod softly. 'And not just because I loved him—I did, Ethan.' Colour floods my cheeks. 'But he made me into something I despise and that took away every good memory. I have no right to look back on any of the fun we had and smile because it was all wrong. *All* of it.'

'I'm sorry,' he murmurs.

And then he kisses me. It's a soft kiss, gentle and slow. An apology and an explanation and it's everything I need. I surrender to it, and in that moment I am weak, because my heart surrenders too.

Later that day my assistant Lesley pops her head into my office. 'Ally?'

I put aside the Christie's brochure I'm leafing through and give her my attention. She's holding a huge bunch of tulips—huge. At least one hundred flowers crammed together and wrapped in brown paper. They are my favourites.

They can't be from Ethan, can they?

The very idea makes adrenalin course in my veins and flavour my mouth. I hope—and I know I shouldn't—that he *has* sent them to me. And yet if he has? I'm scared of that possibility too.

'What are those?' Suspicion is obvious in my tone, my inner conflict apparent in the question.

'Flowers. For you.'

'Who are they from?'

She shoots me a quizzical look. 'I didn't open the card. Do you want me to?'

'No, no, that's okay. I'll do it.'

I take the flowers from her with a dismissive smile and place them on the edge of my desk as if they might burn me.

Lesley is hovering inside the door. I understand her curiosity. Occasionally I get gifts from clients— bottles of whisky or champagne, the odd paperweight.

Never flowers.

And these are my *favourite* flowers.

My heart accelerates as I finger the card. Surely they're not from him? Then again, how can they *not* be?

'Are they from *him*?' Lesley prompts breathily and I realise she's seen it.

She's read the papers. She knows about me and Ethan.

'Thank you,' I say dismissively, sitting down without opening the card.

And, though she's probably still dying to know if they're from him or not, she steps out of my office and closes the door behind her.

I cannot rip the envelope open fast enough. I tear the triangular back and lift the card out, my eyes running over the neat florist's typeface.

Your immortal moral soul is not in danger.

I groan, dropping my head forward. My soul might not be but I think *I* am.

All my good intentions, all my boundaries, are crumbling.

He's leaving soon.

Less than a week.

I need to be strong and then I need to move on.

That's all.

But... Ethan Ash is in my blood, my bones. I see him when I blink and I inhale him with every breath I take. He has become a part of me—and not just of me, but of all that surrounds me.

I reach for my phone on autopilot.

How did you know tulips are my favourite?

I can practically feel him grinning through the phone.

Lucky guess. What time am I seeing you tonight?

I smile as I shake my head. I should say no, but the reminder that he is leaving soon fills me with something like panic.

I finish around six.

His response is swift.

Great. Let's do dinner. I'll pick you up.

My heart races. Dinner? And he'll pick me up? From work?

He texts back before I can respond, before I can demur. After all, dinner is not in our rules. And now, more than ever, I think we need to stick to them.

Don't worry. It doesn't mean anything. It's just more foreplay…

I put my phone into my top desk drawer as though it's a lit stick of dynamite, slamming it emphatically shut. I should be glad.

It doesn't mean anything.

Those words are important. Those words show that he and I are still focused on keeping our boundaries in place. It shows that we can engage in 'high-risk' activities like dinner and flirting and flower-sending-and-receiving and not run the risk of forgetting.

Because it doesn't mean anything. None of this *means* anything. It's just fun.

Panic is what I feel instead of gladness.

I do my best to concentrate on work, but every time I pause my mind wanders to Ethan. To his body. His kisses. To the way he held me all night. To the way he made love to me, hard against the sofa, taking me from behind and playing me more expertly than he does his Fender.

To the way he listened to my heaviest confession and held me tight. Better—to the way he saw past the facts and *understood*. He absolved me of all guilt with one simple smile.

It wasn't my fault.

I couldn't have known.

I reach for my phone almost guiltily and load up Twitter.

He's still trending. My cheeks flush as I click guiltily into the hashtag. The concert videos are still going strong, being re-Tweeted and liked ad nauseam. But there are new photographs as well. Photographs of *us*.

I stare at them and read a few comments, smiling—until I find the comments that are calling me a whore and other less nice things. Someone called *@DreamingOfAsh* really has got a thing against me.

I push out of the thread. It's a timely reminder of why I would never choose to be involved with a man like Ethan. The paparazzi. The fans. The pressure. The constant fear that he'd actually go for one of those groupies after a concert one night.

@SiennaandEthanforever has commented on the pic: *Rebound Fuck.* I smile, pleased on some level that an outsider can identify us for what we are. Yet the smile is brittle, and I find that not *all* of me is pleased by the description, even though it's accurate.

Like watching a train wreck happening before my eyes, I click back into the comments. There are one thousand and twenty-three.

He'll never stay with her. He's always loved Sienna.

Dude, Sienna's engaged to @TheRealTomBanks didn't you see?

Engaged...whatever. This is just to promote her album.

Sienna and Ethan are made for each other. Always have been, always will be.

I can't look away. I click out of Twitter and load up a browser, and before I know what I'm doing my fingers corrupt my intent to remain uninvolved.

Ethan Ash + Sienna Di Giorgio.

I only have to type the 'S' of Sienna's name before I'm prompted with the full name. I click and wait.

In seconds my screen is populated with articles, blogs and pictures. I click hungrily into the first blog. It's by a popular blogger who runs a mostly benign site with occasionally mean-spirited posts about celebrities he's taken it into his head to hate.

Apparently he hates Sienna. And loves Ethan. Which makes me smile again—more naturally this time. The photo on my screen was taken in broad daylight. They're obviously fighting. She's crying, but still looking like a beautiful porcelain doll, and Ethan is looking pissed off.

And sexy.

For a moment I let myself wonder what they were saying, what their fight was about. I can see that Ethan is tired and angry and frustrated and annoyed. I can imagine the roll of his voice as he implores her to be reasonable. I can hear him as though he were standing in front of me.

He looks exhausted, and I want to reach into the photo and smooth away his worries. It's a silly fantasy—one that is out of place in our arrangement.

A shudder runs down my spine, reminding me of the way he dragged his lips down my back, nipping me at the base of my spine before rolling his tongue over the bite mark.

There are new photos of just Ethan, too. From today? Ethan stepping out of the hotel, baseball cap tugged low, covering his eyes. Head bent. Even in the still images I can see the swagger in his step.

Desire throbs in my gut.

I scroll to a concert video and tap to watch it without realising.

It goes full-screen and I press the volume higher, then lean back in my chair to watch. It's from the start of a concert. He's walking on stage and the crowd is going wild. The noise is deafening. He raises his hands in the air in greeting and whoever is filming lifts the camera to the big screen, so that I can see his smile as he lifts his guitar.

He slips the strap over his head, turns to face someone just off stage and nods, then strums the guitar. Once. Loudly.

The crowd erupts.

'How you doing, New York?' he calls, and the crowd's screaming is louder. 'We're gonna have some fun tonight.'

He launches into a song—one of his earlier hits. I

am mesmerised. I watch the whole thing twice, my heart throbbing, my body craving, and then my eyes lift to the tulips.

Tonight can't come soon enough.

'I'm impressed your attention span's lasted this long. She must be *really* in good in bed.'

I stare at the screen in frustration.

'Is there a reason you're Face Timing me, Sienna? Other than to show more than a natural interest in my sex life?'

She swishes her hair over one shoulder—a gesture that used to drive me crazy. I can imagine the way it will smell, like flowers and vanilla. You know that weird way smells have of binding themselves to your core memories and triggering them whenever prompted?

'We were together a lifetime, Ash. Am I not allowed to care about who you're with now?'

I laugh. An instant dismissal. 'Not really.'

I unbutton my shirt, my eyes on hers mockingly. There is a part of me that knows how fucked up this is—that acknowledges I'm playing with fire and that someone's going to get badly burned.

But it won't be me. And I won't let it be Ally.

'So?' Sienna slowly runs her eyes down my body, her admiration something she doesn't bother to hide. 'Is it serious?'

'No.' I grin, but something like pain clutches inside me. 'It's fun. A whole lotta fun.'

'What's *that* supposed to mean?'

I lean closer, so that my face is all she can see. 'It means that Ally and I are having a whole lotta fun. And that's it.'

Tears sparkle in Sienna's eyes and my reaction is instantaneous. *Guilt.*

What am I *doing*? I'm not this guy. I'm not going to flaunt it over my ex that I'm fucking someone beautiful and hot and sexy and distracting. What Sienna did is beyond forgiving, but that doesn't give me a free pass to be an A-grade dick.

Besides, whatever satisfaction I thought I'd get from rubbing my sex-life in Sienna's face is non-existent. What I'm doing is about Ally and me and the way she makes me feel. Sienna is incidental.

'You're engaged,' I say slowly. 'None of this matters.'

'I just…' She wipes away the tears and her lower lip pouts. 'I miss you.'

Fuck.

The words hit me square in the chest—like little missiles that pull me apart from the inside out.

'You miss me?' I repeat, pulling away from my phone and reaching for a fresh shirt.

It is everything I needed to hear a month ago, and yet now those three little words fill me with a chasm of unease. I pull the shirt over my head and come back to the camera. Then I change my mind and pour a measure of Scotch. It's two in the afternoon, but I don't give a shit. In that moment I need something to straighten my head—or to un-straighten it. I need something to calm me down.

'You don't get to call me out of nowhere and say you *miss* me.'

'Don't be angry with me.'

'*Angry* with you?' Incredulity makes my voice sound amused when I'm anything but. 'Are you *kidding* me?'

'I was under so much pressure at the end, you know. The tour and the album... I think I might have...' She shakes her head and leans closer.

I don't know if she deliberately pans the camera down but I can see she's only wearing a bra and lace panties. I look away, the feeling guilt and betrayal of Ally making my breath short.

'I took it out on you. I was such a bitch.'

Yeah. She was. She was a nightmare. But that doesn't change the fact we were together for six years, that I shared twelve years of my life with her—six of them as her lover.

'We'd been growing apart for a long time,' I say, trying to take my share of the blame. 'We spent so much time apart. The end was inevitable.'

'Was it?'

It's a sad question. One full of heartache and hurt.

'*You* ended this. You ended *us*.' I throw the whisky back and place the glass down a little more heavily than I should. 'And you got engaged to Tom.'

'That was a mistake,' she says, and then she sobs.

And those six years spent caring about Sienna, wanting her to be happy, damned well *loving* her, make me forget the hurt she's inflicted.

'Can we go back in time and fix it, Ash?'

* * *

I feel a tiny bit like royalty as I step out of my office onto the busy twilight streets of Manhattan and see a sleek black car waiting for me. Grayson is beside it, dressed in a suit. I flick a smile at him but then I look lower instantly, towards the heavily tinted window of the car, behind which I know Ethan will be sitting.

Just like last time.

My pulse is thready and I feel sensual tension running through me like a powerful car idling at the lights. One hint of green and I will pounce.

I walk slowly, glad I made the effort to slip home at lunch and change into something fresh. I've gone with a black jersey dress that falls to my ankles, with sleeves which bell to my wrists. The neckline is demure, but it hugs me like a second skin.

I love this dress.

Small fact: I destroyed every piece of clothing I owned after Jeremy. Everything. Anything he had seen me in, and obviously anything he'd given me or touched me in—which was pretty much everything. I could no longer bear to associate who I was with who I'd been, and every time I put an outfit on I heard his voice. I felt his hands.

It was, perhaps, the first stage of my eight-month-exorcism—the first step in preparation for this. The final erasing of the man I once loved.

It's silly, I suppose, but I like feeling that no other guy has touched me in this dress.

I like it that it's all for Ethan.

That thought is running dangerously close to breaking our rules, so I fold it away and push a bright smile to my face. It doesn't falter when Grayson opens the door.

I move into the car and Ethan is there, overpowering me with his presence, all that I need, all that I can sense, and he's just sitting there, staring at me.

'Hey.'

He holds a hand out and I reach for it as I step in, sitting beside me. Am I imagining it or is he frowning?

I must be imagining it, because within a minute he smiles at me, and pleasure reaches right down to the bottom of my toes.

'How was your day?' I ask.

He leans forward, brushing his lips to mine. 'Better now.'

'I have a bone to pick with you,' I murmur.

'Yes? What's that?'

'Flowers.' I lift a finger in mock admonishment. 'Flowers are expressly prohibited in our terms of engagement. Clause One, Part A.'

'Ah.' He grins as he catches my finger and brings it to his lips. 'I remember. I'm revising that clause.'

His eyes hold mine and my heart thumps, and I am grateful that Grayson chooses that moment to slide into the driver's seat.

'Where to?' Grayson tosses over his shoulder.

'The hotel?' I whisper in Ethan's ear, smiling conspiratorially.

He laughs, wrapping an arm around me and holding me close to him, keeping me cradled to his side.

'Belle Nuit,' Ethan contradicts, naming one of the hottest eateries in New York.

I've heard of it, of course. It's just over the bridge, hooked into Brooklyn, with a stunning view of the Manhattan skyline—and Brooklyn Bridge.

'Ethan,' I say softly. This is another rule that's being flaunted. 'Why don't we just grab takeout and go back to yours? Or go to Benji's diner…?'

'Because.' His eyes glint as they meet mine. 'This place is nice.'

'Nice?' I roll my eyes. 'It's better than that.'

'Have you been there?'

'Well, no, but I mean it's *the* place…'

'Right.'

'Don't you think it's breaking even more rules?' I push, concern obvious in my question.

'I'm leaving in a few days, Ally. Does it really matter?'

My heart stammers in my chest. *Jesus Christ.* A few days. Something about the finality of that pushes all my stupid objections aside. What can go wrong in a few days?

'I guess not.'

I'm still torn.

His eyes hold mine and my temperature shoots up. Suddenly every touch, every word, is a prelude of what I know will come, and it is hyper-charged with awareness and need. There is a heat between us that is threatening to explode.

Traffic is unusually light, and we cruise over the bridge easily. I look out at the water as we go, admiring the view, thinking what a unique place in the world this is.

The restaurant is as glorious as I imagined. Grayson pulls up right at the front and though it's discreetly decorated, the prestige of the place is marked. There are two waiters standing by the doors, dressed in tuxedos.

One pulls the restaurant door inwards at the same moment Grayson opens the car door, so that it's easy for us to navigate our way in. There are paparazzi—I suspect they're almost permanently camped out at a place like this. Is it stupid to come here?

'My mom's going to have kittens,' I whisper under my breath as we move inside and another waiter appears to lead us to a table.

The place is packed, and I see two newscasters, an actress, and a famous-for-all-the-wrong-reasons Hollywood director and his twenty-something wife tucked away in a corner. We're led to a booth near the windows. It has the advantage of being private and offering an unrivalled outlook of the twinkling lights of Manhattan.

'This is beautiful.'

He nods, but he's distracted. *Again.*

'Does that bother you?' he asks after several long seconds. It takes me a moment to recall what I have said.

'Kind of. Not really.' I shrug. 'She'll get over it. What's one more crime to my name?'

His smile is tight. 'I guess it shows how much she loves you.'

I don't want to talk about my family, though. They're their own unique brand of messed-up. I'll deal with them later. After. Once all this over and I have breathing space to be me again.

'Where do you go after this?'

I ask the question almost as though talking about it will desensitise me to the fact he is leaving. As though it will make the reality more pronounced.

'London.'

'For how long?' *Shit*. Wrong question. It sounds needy.

'A couple of weeks.'

He shrugs and my gut clenches. The idea of a couple of weeks without him is bad enough. Thank God we had the foresight to put limits on this when we did. I imagine being with him for any longer— for another month. Two. Three. And then having to end it. My heart shrivels.

I was supposed to be engaged to Jeremy, and yet I suspect leaving Ethan Ash would be a million times harder and worse. Strange, given how much I loved Jeremy.

Is it just the sex?

I don't know, but I *do* know this is for best. It will still be hard. But it's right to end it now, before we get too attached. Before we do anything stupid like fall in love.

Nothing good can come of love. One day, when

I meet a guy I think I can settle down with, he will be my safe haven, not my storm.

Jeremy was a storm, and Ethan Ash is a cyclone…

CHAPTER THIRTEEN

THIS IS WORK. This is work.

I remind myself of this fact over and over and over again as I head towards Ethan's townhouse. I tell myself to stop remembering the way he made love to me all night.

I mean *all* night. I think I probably got an hour's sleep all in. We didn't leave the restaurant until late. That surprised me. I was so full of need for him, and yet staring across at him, hearing his beautiful husky accent as he talked about his childhood, his family, his *life*, I was mesmerised by the details. I was mesmerised by *him*.

We were the last guests in the restaurant.

I had a glass of Prosecco when we arrived and nothing else, but I felt *drunk* as we left. No, not drunk. High. And so happy.

The second we got back to his hotel we were ripping one another's clothes off.

And I slept over again.

Which makes the trifecta of rule-breaking complete.

But with three days to go—three more days of

possible Ethan Ash consumption—I don't much care. I don't even care that yet another photo of us was running on the gossip sites this morning.

Nor that two of my clients emailed me to ask about my 'relationship' with him.

Nothing can dent my mood. And now I'm here, meeting with Ethan to discuss his art selection, and I'm determined to get through the meeting without doing anything inappropriate. Step one: prove that I can separate sex-life from work-life.

Grayson is waiting out front at Ethan's place. I see him as soon as my cab pulls up.

'Hey.' I smile as I tap up the stairs.

'Miss Douglas.'

'Please, call me Ally.'

He nods. 'Mr Ash is waiting for you.'

Yeah, that's mutual.

'It's cold today, huh?'

His smile is tight. 'Sure is.'

He pushes the door inwards and I move inside, my desire to befriend Grayson instantly consumed by a greater, stronger need to see Ethan. I stride down the hallway and pause just inside the living area.

What the hell…?

First of all, there's furniture. And that's fine. It's great. It's a welcome addition, in fact. But Ethan's interior designer Natasha is also there, smiling at Ethan, nodding as he speaks.

I am mentally removing his clothes, and mine—good intentions be damned—and now we have a lovely third wheel to contend with?

'Ah, Alicia. Wonderful.' She clips towards me with an authoritative air, as though this was her idea—as though I'm meeting her, and Ethan being here is just a happy coincidence.

'Natasha.' I nod, accepting her air kisses even as my eyes lock accusingly with Ethan's. His expression shows bemusement.

'You'll be thrilled to see my progress. Come—have a look,' she invites.

I tamp down on my resentment. She's the designer. She obviously feels a sense of ownership over the project. Her behaviour isn't untoward. It's only my expectations—first of being alone with Ethan and second of being given the tour by *him*, preferably naked and with his hands on my body.

'Great,' I say through gritted teeth.

'You guys get started. I have a few calls to make,' Ethan says.

A few calls to make? *Does* he, indeed?

Natasha shows me the whole downstairs area—and she has done an incredible job. It's beautiful. Artistic while still achieving a degree of homely comfort. The fittings are classic and top-quality and I can see Ethan living here. Relaxing here. It suits him.

My gut twists at the very idea of his inhabiting this space full-time. We move upstairs into another living room, then into a guest room. A bed! *Hallelujah*. Perhaps he'll start spending more time here, rather than at the hotel? He'd be so close to me...

My phone rings and I pause our tour.

'Sorry,' I say, lifting it from my bag, about to decline the call when I see Ethan's name on the screen. 'I'll just be a minute.'

'Take your time. I need to measure the windows again for the drapes,' Natasha answers.

I step out of the room, into the hallway, and swipe to answer.

'Yes?' I snap, conscious that Natasha can probably still hear my end of the conversation.

'You look amazing.'

I turn away, pace a little further down the hallway and lower my voice. 'Thank you. I didn't realise you'd assembled the whole team.'

His laugh is like melted caramel. 'What's the matter? Aren't you having fun?'

'I had a different kind of fun in mind,' I say honestly.

He laughs again. 'Soon. Remember? Foreplay…'

'You're enjoying this.'

'Not as much as I'll be enjoying you, believe me. Have you reached my bedroom yet?'

I lift my head and look down the hallway. 'No. It's next.'

'When you get there I want you to imagine yourself naked in the middle of the bed. Arms outstretched. Fingers curled around the bedposts as I return the favour you gave me at the hotel. I want you to look at that bed and imagine me going down on you until you can barely speak.'

My breath is rushed and I know my cheeks are bright pink. A noise—a creaking floorboard—draws my attention to the stairs. He is walking up them, phone clasped under his ear.

'Think you can do that for me?' he murmurs, his eyes locked to mine.

A slick of need pools between my legs.

Natasha or not, I want to run to him, launch myself at him and strip him naked.

I disconnect the call and slide my phone into my bag, using the act to hide my face and eyes from him.

'Everything okay, Miss Douglas?' he asks as he approaches.

My eyes are wide in my face as I force myself to look at him. 'Oh, perfectly,' I respond, with obvious annoyance.

Except it's not annoyance with him; it's annoyance at not being able to have him. It's desire and white-hot need. It's fierce and uncontrollable and it's consuming me, despite the fact I have not long left his bed.

'Are you sure?'

He brings his body close to mine and pushes me backwards, so that I connect with the wall. We are only metres from the guest room, but he braces himself beside me, partially blocking me from Natasha's view. His fingers move straight to me, touching my most sensitive cluster of nerves through the fabric of my pants.

Did I really think Natasha's being here would stop him—stop this—the inevitability of what we are? He holds my eyes as he moves his fingers in a circular motion, and when I suck in a breath he lifts a finger to my lips.

'Shh,' he says, with a smile on his face.

I don't know if I can be quiet.

I don't know if I can stop this.

I know I should. I know this is unprofessional and that I have a reputation to think about. But I also have a body that is starving for its next fix, and he's offering it to me on a silver platter.

'Come for me, baby. Come without making a sound.'

He moves faster and I press myself down, rolling my hips, begging him with my body to make love to me.

I can feel the orgasm building. I dig my fingernails into my palms to stop myself screaming out, but my silence makes the sensation all the more intense.

Heat is burning me—I am turning to ash.

He sees the moment I explode and he brings his mouth to my ear, buzzing his lips over my earlobe and whispering against me.

'You are perfect.'

I can't catch my breath. I hear Natasha's clip-clopping heels and I step aside from him even as my blood rages like a fever. I suck in air and I spin away, moving towards the window at the end of the corridor, needing a moment to straighten my hair, to collect myself, to calm my body.

'Oh! Ethan.'

It's Natasha.

'Come and have a look at the window treatment options.'

'Nothing I'd like better.'

I hear the grin in his voice and can picture his face even though I'm not looking at him.

It takes me several minutes to calm myself, to begin to feel like I am in control once more. When I'm ready, I move back through the house.

I find them in the master bedroom. Ethan watches me as I walk in, so I know he sees the way my eyes drop to the bed. Immediately. The way colour blooms in my cheeks.

We are both picturing the same thing.

Damn him.

Damn him for knowing how to push my buttons so well.

'What do you think?' Natasha asks excitedly. 'I've gone for a dark oak, because I think it's masculine and classic without being too heavy. Don't you agree?'

'It's perfect,' I murmur, thinking of the art I've selected for this room.

It took me a long time to come up with pieces that I think will suit Ethan. The pieces that I want him to wake up to each morning.

I meet Ethan's eyes for a moment; electricity charges between us.

'I like the bed. Is it a king?'

Natasha takes over. 'Yes. And it's a memory foam mattress. Super-comfortable.'

'Lie down,' Ethan invites, his gaze simmering as it locks to mine. 'See for yourself.'

'That's okay,' I say, a tad more sharply than necessary. 'I've felt mattresses before.'

'Not *this* mattress,' he points out smoothly.

'It really is the best on the market,' Natasha interjects, apparently oblivious to our flirtatious undercurrent.

'How lovely for you,' I murmur, turning to Ethan in time to see him wink at me.

My blood simmers. I think I'm going to turn into a puddle of lava if I don't get out of here.

I reach into my handbag and pull out a printed booklet. 'This is the proposal I mentioned.' I hand it to him. 'Why don't I leave it with the two of you to discuss and I'll follow up with you, Natasha, next week?'

'Excellent,' she agrees, before Ethan can speak, leaving me wondering briefly what he might have said.

'You've done a great job,' I say with an over-bright smile. 'I'll finish the tour another time. Nice to see you both again.'

'You too, Ally.' Natasha reaches across and takes the book from Ethan. 'May I?'

'Sure. Be my guest. I'll walk Miss Douglas out.'

'Please, call me Alicia,' I invite, swaying my hips as I move ahead of him.

He is behind me the whole way. Along the corridor, down the stairs, and then through the hall that leads to his front door. I press my hand around the doorknob, knowing I should say something but not knowing what.

I turn around slowly, but there's nothing slow about the way Ethan moves. He swoops down and kisses me, his whole body pushing mine against the door, trapping me. The weight of him is immovable, his mouth demanding, the intensity of his kiss pressing my head against the door. He grinds his hips and I feel his arousal through our clothes. He kisses me as he holds me captive with his hips, his dick, his very self.

I am powerless to move. I don't want to anyway. I want to do this for ever.

'I'll come to the hotel when I finish work,' I say into his mouth, conscious that we could be interrupted at any point and wanting privacy.

'I won't be there.'

The words don't compute at first.

'Huh?'

'I have a thing,' he says. 'With my manager.' He runs his tongue along my lower lip and I moan. 'Wait for me there.'

I don't think that's a good idea. But before I can say so, he speaks.

'When I come back, I plan to fuck you senseless.'

A shiver runs through me. A frisson of anticipation and need.

Challenge accepted.

'And I'm going to fuck you right back.'

I have no idea what I'm doing.

Ally left an hour ago and I finally got rid of Natasha. Now, ensconced in my basement recording studio, which is coming together slowly, I need to be writing and instead I'm thinking.

About Ally.

About Sienna.

About what the hell I'm doing.

I'm thinking about the fact that I lied to her just now. I have no meeting with my manager. I just wanted to give her a taste of her own medicine. Why is *she* the only one who gets to decide when we see each other?

I'm thinking about the fact that I'm flying out of the States in a matter of days and that if I stick to the rules we agreed to I'm never going to see Ally again. That I was stupid to waste an evening just because I'm pissed off with our boundaries.

I'm thinking about the fact that I hate the thought of not seeing her after I leave. In fact the idea of not seeing Ally makes my skin crawl, and that, in turn, really pisses me off. Because Sienna and I broke up three months ago and, let's face it, it was hardly a clean break. By rights, I shouldn't be obsessing over someone new already, should I? Isn't that disloyal to Sienna and what we were? Maybe. But I'm not sure I have much say in it.

I'm furious at Sienna. No, I hate her. But I loved her once—or thought I did.

And Ally? Where does she fit in to all this? When did convenient sex with no strings start bothering me more than the break-up with the supposed love of my life?

I can't say. I have no idea what I feel for Ally.

But I know that I want her. And that three more days, three more nights with her, is not going to be enough.

I know that I wish we hadn't made those damned rules.

And I know that I'm a rule-breaker from way back. It's time I remembered that.

It's after eleven before I go to the hotel. It's childish, but I feel like it's important to make her wait. Just a bit.

When I step into the suite all thought rattles through me, threatening to drop right out of my head.

Ally is lying on the sofa, wearing a silky negligee, with a book in her hands. *My* book.

'I thought I'd see what all the fuss is about,' she says, and smiles, lifting *Les Misérables* up for me to see.

I had a speech worked out. A plan. I was going to seduce her and then, when she was weakened by desire, I was going to start a conversation. But I've seen her now and I blurt out, 'I'm coming back in a month or so.'

She stands up quickly, her eyes locked to mine.

'What?'

The word is not screeched, and yet it bounces around the room as though it were.

'To New York?' she says after a moment.

'No, to Earth,' I mutter sarcastically. 'Yes. To New York.'

I move further into the apartment. Here it comes. The sentence I've spent days formulating.

'I'd like to see you again.'

Abject fear crosses her face. It is unmistakable.

'What?'

'I'd like to see you again.' I shrug. 'I'll be in London a few weeks. Maybe less. And then I'll fly back here.'

'Why?'

My eyes don't lie. I'm not going to pretend any more. 'Because I'm going to be missing the hell out of you by then.'

She practically jack-knifes across the room, the book in her hand as though it's a lifeline, her tension a palpable force. Silence hangs between us.

'No.'

It's a softly spoken word. It's a plea. And yet it's emphatic.

I brace myself for her argument.

I brace myself for her doubts.

What I don't brace myself for is the fury and rage which is obvious when she spins around a moment later, her eyes pinning me to the spot, burning me with irate contempt.

'How *dare* you?'

It's not what I expect. Did I think she'd be glad? Thrilled? That she's been feeling the same growing sense of disbelief that our arbitrary deadline is drawing closer?

It takes me a moment to shake myself into responding. 'I *dare*—' my words sound coloured with anger '—because I don't want this to end. I'm not ready.'

'Oh, you're not *ready*,' she says sarcastically, slapping her palm to her forehead in an exaggerated and sarcastic gesture of sudden comprehension. '*You're* not ready! How did I dare think you'd do the right thing and stick to our deal?'

'Come on...' I growl the words. 'Be reasonable. We made this deal when we hardly knew each other. Are you telling me nothing's changed for you in the last two weeks?'

Her eyes flash with more anger and her cheeks drain of colour. 'Of *course* things have changed! I'm not an idiot! But nothing *important* has changed. What I want is still the same.'

'And that's for this to end when I leave?'

'Yeah.'

'So if I'm back in New York you really don't want me to call you?'

She frowns, and that little divot forms between her brows. I ache to lift a finger to it and touch it, touch her. But I don't.

'No.'

A laugh escapes my mouth. A sound of disbelief. 'I'm not ready to walk away from you.'

'This isn't about you.'

Her eyes hold mine for a moment and then drop. 'What is it about, then?'

'It's about knowing we need to let this go.'

'Why? You don't think there's something here worth keeping hold of?'

She sniffs.

Hell, is she *crying*? I can handle almost anything, but not Ally's tears. I feel like my chest has been ripped open and someone is reaching in and squeezing my organs in a fist.

I wait for her to answer, my question sitting between us like an enormous, impossible-to-navigate boulder.

'Ally?' I prompt gruffly when she doesn't answer.

'I'll admit,' she says shakily, 'that things between us are kind of amazing—'

'"Kind of amazing"?' I interrupt, running a hand through my hair.

'But it doesn't change the fact that I don't want to be in a relationship. I don't want a boyfriend. I don't want to live with the risks that are bound up in loving someone.'

'So you're—what? Going to stay single for ever? Run through a succession of fuck buddies for the rest of your life?'

The very idea is curdling my blood.

She looks away from me and my stomach drops. *Good job, jackass.* Bully and berate her into a relationship. That's a *great* idea.

'I don't know.'

Her whisper is a plaintive cry. I can't help it. I cover the distance between us, my stride long. I press my body to hers, trapping her with my legs as my hands reach up and lock her face between them. I drag her up as I push my head down, finding her lips as though the survival of humanity will be ensured by this kiss.

'I *know* enough for both of us.'

She shakes her head, and I can taste her tears, and it makes me want to fuck her so much more. It's the only way we can communicate without doubts.

I push at her negligee, my hands demanding, my need raw. I rip it from her body and she moans into my mouth. I drop my lips to her shoulder and taste her flesh with my tongue, then press my teeth into her. She arches her back and, fuck, I need her more than I ever have.

I push at her bra—it's just a scrap of lace that barely holds her in place. I drop it with an equal mix of contempt and admiration, and then I take a breast into my mouth with a primal moan of need.

I cannot function without her.

I lift her, wrapping her legs around me, and she is running her hands through my hair, tasting me, kissing my cheek, my jaw, her hands touching every square inch of me as she goes. I ache to possess her, but this torturous lead-up is heaven on earth.

I drop her onto the bed. I'm not gentle. She bounces as she lands and her eyes contain the same rush of fury as they meet mine.

I don't care.

I'm furious as well. I'm furious with her for sticking to some stupid rules we agreed to way back when we hardly knew each other. But her crying... Her crying damned near breaks my heart.

I don't think she even realises she's doing it, but

I run my tongue along her cheek, catching a tear, tasting her salt and her sadness, and then I kiss her.

I drop my mouth to her chest, running my tongue over her, and my fingers brush her sides, pausing at her hips to hold her as I take my tongue to her clit and torment her in the way I know she loves. Her fingers are tearing through my hair. She lifts her legs and I grip her ankles, holding her there, making her fall apart.

And she does.

She cries out as the rapture of her orgasm drops over us both and then I move, stepping out of my jeans, hovering over her. I stretch across and grab a condom from my side of the bed. My fingers are shaking as I stretch it over me. Need is like a spring, coiled tight in my chest.

I stare at her and, fuck it, I know I need to roll the dice.

I gamble. I gamble in the only way I can think of because I'm all in.

CHAPTER FOURTEEN

'I LOVE YOU.'

The words drop over me as he thrusts into me, his possession complete. I reject the words at the same time as I welcome him. I am fevered and frantic, afraid and so aware of every pulsing need inside my body.

He grabs my hands, lacing his fingers through mine and pinning them wide on either side of my head. His eyes stare down at me.

He thrusts again, harder, deeper, and he says it again.

'I love you.'

He drops his mouth and kisses the words into me, swirling them into me, pushing them through me as he moves, each three-word bomb detonating in time with his body's possession, so that I am being stirred to the height of desire even as I want to scream and push him away. Even as I am terrified and innately rejecting his sentiment.

'Don't!' I say, sobbing, and he pauses, his body still, as if I'm rejecting the sex.

I'm not. The sex is what I want.

'Don't say that.'

'I love you,' he challenges, his eyes locked to mine. Something inside me flutters. Hope? Pleasure? Relief?

But I shake my head. 'This isn't love.'

He thrusts into me again. 'It is for me.'

I shouldn't be able to function in the midst of this, and yet I'm climbing higher and higher. My body is so sensitive that even the air around me is making me shiver with awareness. I can feel it waving over my body. I arch my back, tilting my hips, and he moves inside me again.

'I love you.'

I don't fight it. I don't reject the words. I let them fill me up. I let them curl around my heart and for a moment I pretend they're what I want. Just for a moment.

It is a coming together ruled by animalistic passion, and yet there is a raw emotionalism to it as well. His fingers squeeze mine as we come together, and he kisses me, and I know what he's thinking without him saying it.

He loves me.

Words that so many people find joyous and welcome fill me with dread. They are tainted by past misuse and all its negative associations. Ethan tells me he loves me but I hear Jeremy, and I instantly recall the disaster that followed.

I lie beneath Ethan, his weight on me, his body beautiful and warm, strong and hard. I feel his warmth and strength and I wish it would bleed into me. I am going to need to be strong.

'Excuse me.'

The words come out cold and crisp. He's still inside me and suddenly I need space and I need it now.

All I can think, as his words hover in the air like deceptive little bullets, is what an asshole he is. Why would he *do* this? Love is not why I'm here! Love is not what I want!

I pull my hands; he doesn't argue. I push at his chest and roll him away from me, out of me, and then I stand up in one movement. I am shaking with desire and with anger. My negligee is ripped so I grab one of his shirts. It smells like him and my chest groans under the weight of certainty that soon it will be all I have of him.

'What are you doing?' he asks, watching me as I step into my jeans without bothering to put my undies back on. I tuck them into the back pocket and then run my hands through my hair.

'What do you think?' I respond with the same arctic chill.

'Listen.' He stands, the word soothing and gentle. 'Don't run off.'

I glare at him. 'Does it *look* like I'm running off?'

'Yeah.'

'I'm not,' I snap back, storming into the lounge area and scooping up my bag.

I'm struck by the similarities to that first morning when I said goodbye to him—when I thought it would be the last goodbye.

I push my clutch under my arm and am instantly steadied by its presence. 'I'm walking away.'

'Alicia…' he groans, and when I spin back to him I see he's pulled a pair of low-slung jeans on. They sit on his hips, so I can see the protrusion of where his bones meet the sinew and strength of his shape.

It dries my mouth.

I have kissed every part of him. And I'll never touch him again.

'Don't.' It's a shaky, hollow plea. 'Don't say it again. If it's really how you feel, then please respect that I don't want to hear it.'

'You love me too,' he says, prowling towards me.

'No!' I deny it on every level except one. Deep in my heart I wearily admit the truth of what he's said.

He kisses me gently. 'Yes.'

And, infuriatingly, I feel him smile against my mouth.

I stamp my foot down on his. 'No.'

He rips his mouth away in surprise, his eyes laughing when they meet mine. 'What the hell…?'

But then he's back, kissing me again, holding me to him, holding me tight.

'You love me. And I know that you're not ready to see that, or to say it. But I think you feel it. I'm not going to walk away from this.'

I make a shuddering noise, as though I'm hyperventilating.

'I'm not going to crowd you either. I'm just going to be in your life until you're ready.'

That same little kernel in my heart is jumping up and down. I ignore it.

'Why?' It's a question loaded with suspicion.

'Because this is special. I know that you've been hurt and that you're shit-scared to trust someone again. But I'm not Jeremy. And I love you.'

'He—'

'Didn't love you,' Ethan murmurs. 'No guy who really loved someone could do what he did.'

He shrugs, and the simple truth is sitting between us like a diamond I never noticed before.

It makes so much sense.

Jeremy *never* loved me.

It is so simple and so immediately freeing.

Except there's nothing simple about the tangle of what I'm feeling now.

I'm still so angry. I'm angry at Jeremy and at Ethan, and I'm angry at myself for letting it get this far.

'I need to go,' I say.

'Alicia,' he says grimly. 'Don't walk away from this.'

I storm towards the door and wrench it inwards. I have no concept of what I feel, nor of what I want. I know only that I need to get away from Ethan before I start actual ugly crying.

'I have to go.' I force myself to meet his eyes. 'I'm sorry.'

I don't sleep. I brood. Ally has left me after I put everything on the line. Ally has left me after I did everything I could to help her see why she should stay.